THE SIGNET RING

By

Sharon Garrison

THE SIGNET RING

A Novella

CHAPTER ONE

It had been the practice of Mr. Thomas Bennet to send one of his two elder daughters to London to visit their aunt and uncle, the Gardiners. One spring was Elizabeth's turn; she was younger of the two, and while she was there her aunt took her to a tea given by Lady Aylesbury. While at the tea Elizabeth met a young lady four years her junior and they communicated quite well for being such strangers to each other. The young lady's aunt was so impressed with Elizabeth's ability to bring the girl out of her shyness that she arranged for the two of them to meet frequently while Elizabeth was in town. When the visit was coming to an end, the girls determined to write to each other. They had been corresponding with each other for a year when Elizabeth received the following missive, which was sent by courier.

August 12, 1811

Dear Elizabeth,

As you know, my brother has gone to Ireland to conduct business there and I am left here in

Derbyshire dying of boredom from having no one to speak to except my companion, Mrs. Annesley. You know I cannot confide in her as I can with you. Can you find it in your heart to come to Pemberley for a visit of some two months?

Please send a message by my courier telling me whether or not you can come. If you can, I can send a coach to come and get you, and send you back when your visit comes to an end. I beg of you to rescue me from my sea of ennui.

Your Friend, G. Darcy

Elizabeth took the letter to her father and asked if she might go to Pemberley for two months. She let him read the letter and he thought for a while. "You are aware that Derbyshire is quite a distance away from here and you will have to stay at inns for two nights. I would worry about your safety."

"Whenever Georgie travels, she has a contingent of armed postilions, drivers, and footmen. I could also take a maid with me and have her stay in the room with me."

"We can scarcely spare one of the maids here. If I allow you to go, take one of your sisters."

"I will ask Jane if she would like to go. She did not go to the Gardiners this year because of illness and I think she would like to meet Georgiana."

"If Jane will go with you, I will allow the trip. She is dependable and will know what to do during your travels. If she agrees, send a positive response to your friend."

"Thank you, Papa." Elizabeth stood and gave him a kiss on the cheek and then left the study to find her sister. She found her in the stillroom arranging flowers in a vase. Elizabeth approached Jane and said, "Jane, I have an invitation to go to Pemberley in Derbyshire to visit my friend Georgiana. Will you go with me?"

"Oh, yes, Lizzy. I would love to go. I have wanted to meet her for these many months."

"I must write my acceptance now. She will let us know when to expect the coach." Elizabeth ran off to her room to write her response and she explained that she would be traveling with her sister. She gave the message to the courier, who was in the kitchen drinking a tankard of ale and eating a sandwich. When he finished his repast he hopped on his horse and galloped away in a cloud of dust.

While waiting for Georgiana's reply, the two girls looked through their wardrobes and decided what they would need to pack for the trip. A few things required some mending, so they busied themselves for a while doing that. The next day they went into Meryton and purchased some new ribbons, stockings, and a petticoat for each of them.

By the sixth day a reply arrived telling them to expect the coach on Wednesday of that week. The coach would be coming from London, so it would arrive by ten in the morning. This gave them one day to get everything packed into their trunks and for Mr. Bennet to decide how much money to allow them for the trip.

Elizabeth opened up her treasure box and lifted out a pouch of money she had saved over time and she placed it a purse in the bottom of her trunk. She had last month's allowance in her reticule to pay for incidentals during the visit. Jane had some of her allowance left also, so she would take it as well.

In the midst of all the packing, Mrs. Bennet came in the room. "Lizzy how is it that you could only take Jane with you? It seems you could have taken Lydia with no trouble at all to anyone. I am sure you will meet some eligible bachelors on your journey and I know neither of you will make the most of it."

"I chose Jane because she is of age and can make decisions that I cannot. Papa said I could take one sister with me, and I also told Georgiana to expect but one. She is not expecting anyone else. It would be rude to show up with two sisters."

"I will speak to your father."

Mrs. Bennet did so, but Mr. Bennet steadfastly refused to send Lydia with her two elder sisters. He knew Lydia would be nothing but a problem for them and they would get no enjoyment from their trip.

That night neither of them got any sleep. They chatted the whole night through about their expectations for the journey. In the morning both of them put a couple of books in their valises to read on the coach during the trip. They also included some embroidery supplies for later use and their sketchbooks.

Elizabeth was up by six, and she dressed first. She went down to the breakfast room while Jane dressed. Mr. Bennet was at the table consuming his meal and he asked Elizabeth if she had everything she needed. Elizabeth knew what he was referring to and answered in the affirmative.

Jane joined them and sat down to her breakfast and the two girls ate their meals. When they were finished Mr. Bennet handed Jane a pouch with funds for their stays at the inn and for meals. "Did you two think of gifts for any personal servants you may have?"

"Yes, Papa. We have handkerchiefs that we will embroider and we plan to put a coin in each one to give to the servants."

"So you seem to have thought of everything. I will have Mr. Hill bring down your trunks. You two stay near the house in the event the coach arrives earlier than stated."

It did turn out that the coach was earlier than planned, but the girls were quite ready. A footman alighted and loaded the trunks and the girls put on their spencers and bonnets. They grabbed their valises and reticules and Mr. Bennet handed them into the coach. He stood and watched as the coach moved on and waved as the girls waved back.

As expected there were two coachmen, two postilions and the footman. On the first day of the journey, they stopped at eleven to change horses and stopped again at three to change them again. At the second stop, the girls left the coach to refresh themselves and to purchase cups of tea and a roll to consume, which satisfied them until dinner.

The last stop was at quaint little inn where they stopped for the night. The employees at the inn seemed to know the drivers and postilions so Elizabeth thought that the Darcys on their journeys north used this inn quite frequently.

The footman, Mr. Jamieson, showed the ladies to their rooms where they washed their hands and faces and adjusted their hairpins. When they were ready they went to a private parlor that had been ordered for them. There they had a dinner of vegetable soup, some fish, and an assortment of breads, butter, and for dessert pieces of apple pie. To drink they had mugs of small beer and cups of tea. When Jane asked how they were to pay for their stay at the inn, she was told that it had been taken care of by Miss Darcy. Nevertheless, they left a shilling on the table for the servant. The service in this inn was very good in all respects and the girls had no reason to complain.

That night was the first night either of them had slept at an inn. The novelty of it appealed to them until late that night they heard the snores of another guest in the room next door. The girls giggled, put pillows over their heads and tried to go back to sleep, but to no avail. When the sun rose they gave up trying to sleep, so they arose and washed up and got dressed.

A maidservant tapped on the door a little later and asked if they needed anything and she let them know that breakfast would be ready in half an hour.

Jane dressed Elizabeth's hair and Elizabeth did the some for Jane. They packed away their nightclothes and looked around to see that they had everything. While they ate their breakfast of porridge, toast and fruit the footman took their trunks and valises to the coach.

On the first leg of that day's journey, the girls fell asleep until the coach stopped for the first change of horses. While that was going on they got out of the coach to stretch their legs. They saw a sweet shop across the street, so they walked over to purchase some sweets to take with them. They offered some to the drivers and they accepted one piece each. The footman and postilions said, "No, thank you."

Elizabeth asked the one driver how much further was it to their destination when they stopped for the third time that day. He said they were now over the Derbyshire border but still had about fifty more miles to go before reaching Pemberley. They should reach Pemberley by two in the afternoon.

That night the girls slept much better than the night before, but a crying baby awakened them before sunrise the next morning. After breakfast the trunks and valises were loaded and they took off for the third and last leg of the journey. By that afternoon Elizabeth had had enough of sitting in a coach and would have gotten out to run the last few miles if she knew the direction. Even Jane was weary of travel and the inability to stretch when necessary.

At the last change of horses the driver told Elizabeth they were now on Pemberley grounds but it would take another two hours to go around by road to the estate house. Elizabeth did not realize the estate property was so large, although she had heard rumors that Mr. Darcy was quite well off, but she had no real idea of this economic status and had no real desire to learn of it.

The rest of the way they left the window shades open so they could see the passing scenery. It was rugged in places, with immense forests hiding some of the views. Elizabeth thought the scenery she was able to see was beautiful if a little wild. She felt she could spend days exploring the wilderness and the overlooks that would expose meadows and farms.

"Jane, what do you think of this topography?"

"It appears to be quite wild, but varied. We are, I think, in a valley now for I believe we are beginning to enter rising ground. I hardly know what we will find before us."

"We are in the peak district so driving up and down hills and mountains is to be expected. We are not very far from the Lake District. I would dearly love to go there some day."

The coach continued to climb until it reached a flat ridge that overlooked the home grounds of the estate. Jane noticed it first and grabbed Elizabeth's hand. "Lizzy, look over here quickly!"

Elizabeth looked out Jane's window and gasped, "Are we going there? I did not know our destination would be a palace!"

"I hardly know if I am up to staying in such grandeur. What can we do, Lizzy?"

Elizabeth took Jane's hand and pressed it. "We can only be on one room at a time, so we will take the days as they come to us. I am sure Georgie will have everything all planned for us, so we will have no time to be nervous."

After another twenty minutes they arrived at the manor house where Georgiana was eagerly awaiting her guests on the portico. The footman opened the door to the coach and handed the two women out. They were scarcely out of the coach when Georgiana rushed up and hugged

Elizabeth as though she had not seen her in years. Elizabeth introduced Jane and Georgiana was delighted to greet her and said, "Your sister is gorgeous, Lizzy."

Jane blushed rosily, "I thank you for allowing me to come with my sister. I have wanted to meet you for many months now."

"It is my pleasure to welcome my dear friend's sister. Now I shall have two friends to keep me company while my brother is away. Nothing could please me more. Come now, and let me introduce you to our housekeeper. She can help you with any problems you incur while you are here. She will show you to your rooms and see that you are brought some tea and biscuits. Take your time refreshing yourselves. Dinner will be served at half past five this evening. We do not dress for dinner unless there is a party of twenty or more and we shall not have any of that while you are here."

Inside, Georgiana handed the women over to Mrs. Reynolds, who cheerfully led them to their assigned rooms. Georgiana had ordered that they be given rooms in the family wing. Each room was complete with a bedchamber and dressing room, which were connected by a shared sitting room. Maids were busily emptying the trunks and putting things away.

Elizabeth's room was decorated in blues and greens and Jane's was done up in white and pink. Mrs. Reynolds explained, "Just across the hall is Miss Darcy's chamber. You must call for a maid to send any requests to the kitchens or to ask for any assistance. I shall always be at your service."

"Mrs. Reynolds, I believe both my sister and I could use some tea to slake our thirst."

"I shall see to it immediately. For the present, baths are being prepared for the both of you in your dressing rooms. Miss Darcy will come to fetch you before dinner time."

Elizabeth smiled, "Thank you, Mrs. Reynolds."

Jane went to her room and Elizabeth went to her room. The maid offered to help Elizabeth out of her gown and assisted her into the tub, which was behind a painted screen. The screen had a picture of lambs in a field of clover. It was pretty.

While Elizabeth bathed the maid pressed the gown for Elizabeth to wear that evening. Elizabeth felt good in the warm water and soaked before washing herself. She was so tired that she almost fell asleep. She roused herself and finished washing. She had never been in such a large tub before; it was so luxurious. When she was finished with her bath, the maid handed her a large Turkish towel, which she wrapped around her and Elizabeth patted herself dry after she stepped out of the tub. When dry she donned her robe and tied it around her waist.

Elizabeth asked the maid, "What is your name?"

"I am Janice and my sister is Ally. She is your sister's maid."

"Thank you, Janice."

Elizabeth donned her shift and her petticoat and Janice sat her charge on the stool before the dressing table. She took the pins from her hair and brushed it until it shone, then began to take sections to wrap and pin into to place. When done, she left one lock to hang over Elizabeth's left shoulder. Elizabeth then stepped into her gown and Janice fastened the buttons. "Janice, I have never had my hair done this way. I like it very much. You are very good at hairdressing."

"It is a pleasure to work with you, Miss Elizabeth. Your hair is so soft and wavy; many women would give a fortune to have such hair."

It is kind of you to say so. Thank you for your assistance." Elizabeth put on her slippers and Janice went back into the dressing room to complete putting away Elizabeth's things and to press the rest of her gowns.

Elizabeth went into the sitting room and knocked on her sister's door. Ally answered the knock and allowed Elizabeth to enter the room.

"Miss Elizabeth, your sister will be ready soon. If you wish you may wait in the sitting room or in here."

"I shall wait in the sitting room. Thank you." Elizabeth walked through to the sitting room and looked around to find a settee arranged against the long wall, an escritoire to the right of the outer door. Two small tables were placed on either side of the settee, and one chair before the escritoire. A small bookcase stood to the left of the outer door. There were some books in it and Elizabeth examined the titles. Some she had read and others she had not. She chose one to begin that evening, and history of Italy, written in Italian. She knew some Italian and wanted to see if she could make sense of the book. She was looking at the first chapter when she heard a knock at the outer door. She opened it and Georgiana was on the other side.

"Come in, Georgie. Jane will be ready in a moment."

"I love the way your hair has been done. I must paint you with your hair down some day when you are wearing that gown. It becomes you so well. Will you sit for me?"

"It would be my pleasure to do so. But, if I sit for you, you must sit for me."

"Does your sister Jane paint and draw?"

"Jane can paint landscapes, but she has not mastered portraits. I, on the other hand, am better at drawing portraits than landscapes. I think between us we could to one good painting. Both of us can draw adequately, however, and our sister Catherine is very good at any type of art. She is familiar with water colors and oils."

17

"After dinner, I will show both of you my studio. My brother has one as well."

"I was not aware that your brother painted, Georgie. But, then, I know very little about him anyway."

"Indeed he does. He is shy about letting anyone know about it, though. When he was younger Mr. Wickham used to tease him when he was working on a drawing or painting."

"Who is Mr. Wickham?"

"He is the son of my father's late steward. The senior Mr. Wickham was a good man and a fine worker. My father admired him very well. When he died my father took care of his son, sent the boy to Eton with my brother and later to Cambridge, but the younger Wickham did not appreciate what was done for him.

"When my father died, he came to William and demanded his inheritance, which my bother gave him. My father also left him the living at Kympton, but he determined he did not wish to be a churchman, so he agreed to take three thousand pounds in lieu of the living. In no time at all he had wasted his inheritance, every pence of it by gambling and profligate living. I know not all the sins he had committed, but they were grave. On top of all that he tells lies about my brother."

"Why would he do that?"

"Heaven knows why. I have never understood the man and I have known him all of my life. He even tried to elope with me, but brother was there to rescue me. For this reason I travel with armed guards, just as I had provided for you and your sister."

"So the footman and postilions were really guards?"

"Yes, they were."

"In that case, I must thank you for thinking of our safety. I knew already you traveled with guards but I thought it was because your brother was being extra careful of you."

"He is that, Elizabeth. I caution you if you wish to walk about outside, take a guard with you. I can assign one, if you like."

"Do not worry, I have no wish to cause you any anxiety and I will be careful and have a guard go with me on my rambles."

Finally, Jane came into the sitting room, apologizing for her delay. A broken strap on her stays caused it. Now that they were all together, Georgiana led her friends out into the hall and down to the sitting room on the next floor. There they would wait for the dinner to be announced.

"We will be dining in the breakfast room during your stay, since it is more cozy than the formal dining room. We usually only take meals in there when we have house full of guests. There will be only four of us."

Elizabeth assumed the fourth diner would be Mrs. Annesley, but she was wrong, for a stocky, tousle-haired gentleman in regimentals entered the room. "Georgie, will you introduce your guests to me."

"Richard, these are my friends, Miss Jane Bennet and her sister Miss Elizabeth Bennet. Ladies, this is my cousin, Colonel Richard Fitzwilliam."

"It is a pleasure to meet both of you. Will you have a long visit?"

"We have arranged to stay for two months. By then, Georgiana's brother will have returned to keep her company."

"Richard, I begged Elizabeth to come to me and she asked if she might bring her sister since her father would not allow her to come so far all alone. Please have a seat, dear, for dinner will not be ready for another few minutes."

Richard sat down and began to speak, "Did you have a nice trip, ladies?"

"It was the first time either of us had traveled so far. We have often been to London, but no further. We were on the road for three days and spent two nights at inns along the way. That was a new experience for us as well. We knew not what to expect that first night. We shared a room and the accommodations were quite comfortable. But late that night someone in the next room began to snore so we had to put pillows over our heads, which did not work as well as we had hoped. The second night was better, but then a crying baby awakened us early. I must say, the food was very good in both places."

Richard laughed, "Snoring and crying babies are hazards for a good night's sleep. I hope you are not bothered by either tonight."

They all laughed and then Georgiana asked, "Did either of you bring riding habits?"

Elizabeth looked at Jane, who shook her head, "I am afraid we did not bring them. Had you planned to go riding?"

"Since Richard is here, I thought we could do so. I could supply you with the habits for I have several that do not fit me any more. I am sure I can find one for each of you, and perhaps they will need minimal fitting."

"If it causes no trouble, we would be pleased to go riding with you. I am not as accomplished as Jane, but I can ride."

"Excellent, we shall plan to ride the day after tomorrow. We can get the habits fitted tomorrow and after dinner this evening I plan to give you two a tour of the house. Would you like to accompany us, Richard?"

"It would be my pleasure, Poppet. And might there be any music after the tour?"

"I dare say there may be some. Elizabeth can play very well, and I have heard her sing. She had a lovely soprano voice. Do you play, Miss Bennet?"

"I am afraid I have not the talent to play the pianoforte, but I can sing. Elizabeth and I often sing with our sisters."

In that case we shall all have to sing this evening. Richard sings a lovely baritone to my alto range. By the way, Richard, did brother send you to check on me?"

The Colonel cleared his throat and answered, "Actually, it was mother who sent me. She heard that Fitzwilliam was going to Ireland and was leaving you here. She did not like thinking that you would be all alone."

"As you see, I am not all alone. I should have written to her and let her know of my plans. The Bennets can stay for a full two months."

"Yes, I see. It is too bad they did not bring a brother with them."

"Colonel that would have been impossible, for we have no brothers. Men are in short supply in our family. Recently we lost the only male cousin in the family, who was the heir to our father's estate, a Mr. William Collins," explained Elizabeth.

The Colonel raised his eyes, "Did you say William Collins? Was he by any chance a vicar?"

"He was. He had the living at a parish in Kent."

"It is, indeed, a small world. Collins had the living in our Aunt de Bourgh's parish. Fitz and I met him last year at Rosings. What happened to him?"

Elizabeth thought a bit before responding, "I heard that he had gone out to go fishing and accidently fell into the creek. He could not swim so he panicked and his heavy coat got soaked and dragged him down. The creek was in full flow at the time, so it was rather deep. Unfortunately, he did drown."

"I am assuming the estate was entailed to the heirs male, am I correct?"

"Yes, Colonel, you are correct in your assumption. There are no more heirs male in the family, so that puts us in quite a quandary. Perhaps the estate will be taken by the crown when our father passes."

"Should you or one of your sisters marry and have a male child, would that child be eligible to inherit the estate?"

"I hardly know. What I do not quite understand is how Mr. Collins had become the heir, for he was not a Bennet. Wiser minds than mine must investigate that problem."

The last course was served and eaten when Georgiana rose to indicate the meal was over. The all met in the hall and Georgiana suggested they begin their tour of the house before they lost all the light for the day. They began on the top floor, which gave them the opportunity to see the art studio. On the way they went through the portrait gallery to a second set of stairs to the upper floors. They took a few moments to look at the portraits and Elizabeth was surprised to see someone she had seen in town last year.

"Georgie, who is this?"

"That is my brother. Do you know him?"

"No, I do not, but I believe I have seen him in town a few times. One time we bumped into each other at a bookstore and I dropped my selections and he kindly picked them up for me. I begged his pardon and he bowed and walked off. I am sure it was your brother."

"Would it not be amusing if it were him. Come let us go to my studio now." They walked up the staircase to the third floor, which was composed of a nursery, schoolroom, and rooms for the governess or nanny. These rooms were currently not in use. The studios were located at the end of the hall, Georgiana's studio to the left and another for Mr. Darcy to the right. The end of this wing faced east and caught the morning light very well.

In Georgiana's studio there were three easels, a drafting table, a number of stools, shelves to hold jars and tins of paint, brushes, paper, canvases, and other painting and drawing supplies. A stack of finished paintings leaned against the wall.

"Georgiana, may I look at these paintings?"

"Yes, certainly."

Elizabeth flipped through the artwork and Jane stood beside her and looked over her shoulder. "These are lovely, Georgiana. Do you plan to have them framed?"

"Some day in the future I shall do so. Over here is an especially made case to hold all my flat drawings. My brother has several of the chests."

"This is a beautiful piece of furniture and of a good size. For your brother to need three must mean he is prolific painter."

"If no one tells him, I can show some of his works to you." As they closed up Georgiana's studio she took a key from the top of the doorjamb of the opposite studio, "Remember, this never happened."

Four chests like the one in the other studio stood side by side in a much larger room. There were also three easels and one of them had a painting in progress on it.

"Miss Elizabeth, would you come over here for a moment and look at this painting?" asked the Colonel.

She walked over to the easel and looked on in astonishment to see the image of her looking back. "My word that is a painting of me! How could this be?"

"You say he bumped into you. He must have been impressed with the way you looked that day."

"It may be sir, but I was not wearing that gown on that day. At least I was happy then."

"He does have your eyes done well. I can see the humor in them."

"Thank you, Colonel."

"Let us be going downstairs to finish the tour. I hope brother comes when you are still here and see how he reacts to seeing you."

They went to the second floor and Georgiana explained that the family wing was to the east and the guest rooms were in the west wing. Since their father's death they had few guests stay there, except on occasion for Mr. Bingley to come for a time. But that was not often, for he would once and a while bring his sisters and brother-in-law with him. Georgiana was never comfortable with them.

On the first floor they toured the ballroom, which took the length of the entire west wing, with anterooms along the one side of the room. The drawing room was in the east wing and a sitting room was across the hall, and one beside the drawing room. The family used the larger one exclusively and the other smaller sitting room was used for visitors who were waiting to see one of them. Further along the hall was Mr. Darcy's study, another small sitting room, and at the end was a set of double doors, behind which was the library. Elizabeth was amazed at the size of the library for it was two stories high. There must be another entrance to it on the ground floor. She could the stairway to the lower level and the floor of the upper level encircled the room allowing people to access the books shelved there.

They walked down the central staircase to the lower floor and Elizabeth could see the exit door to the left, which appeared to lead outside to the gardens. There was along one wall tall windows to let in the light and window seats were built into each niche. On either side of each window were ceiling high bookcases. A number of step stools and ladders were available for those who would wish to reach the top of the shelves. Elizabeth thought she would stay there for years and never see everything.

"You may never get Elizabeth out of here," said Jane.

They went back up the stairs and Georgiana showed Elizabeth a secret door that led to a tucked away reading room. "My brother likes to go in there when he needs solitude. It often happens when he has a lot on his mind and does not wish to the interrupted.

Everyone except Elizabeth walked to the door to exit the room. She still stood there in awe, but Jane called to her to come with them. "Lizzy, come along, you can spend some time here at another time."

Their final stop was the formal dining room before going to the music room to spend some time playing and singing. There was also a billiard room near the formal dining room, but the ladies did not care to see it, for it was a gentleman's domain.

In the music room Georgiana looked through some music, showed it to Elizabeth and Elizabeth nodded her approval. Georgiana played and Elizabeth sang the lyrics. To include Jane in the musical evening, Elizabeth chose a piece that Jane knew well and invited her to sing along with her as she played. Georgiana then urged the Colonel to join in on a quartet while she played the music.

"Colonel, I am impressed with your musical ability. Is it a prerequisite to becoming an officer?"

"No, Miss Elizabeth, but dancing is a prerequisite to becoming one of Wellington's staff."

"I believe I have heard of that truism."

"I am pretty sure you ladies must be exhausted from your journey. It would not offend me if you wish to go to bed now."

"Miss Darcy, I will take you up on that. I am quite tired. Elizabeth, on the other hand, has more stamina than I, so she may wish to be up longer."

"Do you want me to call a maid to guide you to our room, Miss Bennet."

"Please do. I am sure I will get lost if I go up alone."

Georgiana called for the maid and gave her the necessary instructions and Jane left with her. Georgiana also directed that tea be brought to the sitting room. The three remaining went to the sitting room and the women made themselves comfortable. The Colonel excused himself to tend to some correspondence. Elizabeth and Georgiana took their tea and chatted companionably.

"Lizzy, I noticed you have a hearty appetite, but you never seem to gain weight. How do you manage that?"

"I suppose it may be because I walk a great deal, and even when I do not have the

28

opportunity to walk, I manage to stay the same. Apparently I have a different constitution than many do. I really cannot explain it any further."

"I have quite a number of activities planned, so I hope your sister will be able to keep up with us."

"What do you have in mind?"

"Besides going through my riding habits, I thought we could survey the gardens for a while and perhaps go into Lambton later in the afternoon tomorrow. I have a little shopping to do and I would like to show you around the town."

"That sounds like a fine plan, Georgie."

"On Sunday, we shall go to church and perhaps ride in the afternoon. Monday, we can begin to draw what we wish to paint."

While the two ladies were discussing activity plans, the Colonel pulled out some writing paper from his traveling lap desk and began to write.

August 29

Darcy,

Mother learned you had gone to Ireland on business and was anxious about Georgiana being left behind. She asked me to come to Pemberley to check on your sister to see if she were doing well. Can you imagine my surprise when I found out that two gorgeous women were here at Georgiana's behest?

I am not exaggerating when I say the women are gorgeous. One is a beautiful blonde with a sweet temperament. She has dreamy blue eyes and a flawless, creamy complexion. Her sister is petite and has wavy dark hair, large dark brown eyes with lighter flecks that sparkle in the light. She looks as though she likes to be outdoors a lot, for she has charming freckles across her pretty little nose. She has an outgoing personality and I understand she is Georgie's long-time friend. She has already fallen in love with your library.

If I were you I would hurry back home and stake my claim. Rush through your business before all this loveliness has to go back home. They plan to be here for a full two months.

By the way, I have leave for a month, but with these beauties before me, I believe I will be arranging a courtship with one before much more time elapses. Since you prefer brunettes, perhaps I shall choose the blonde.

Richard.

He folded and sealed the letter, wrote the direction and laid it aside to begin another to his mother who was at Matlock with his father.

August 29,

Dearest Mother,

30

I arrived at Pemberley in good time and found Georgiana is well, much as I expected. She has two guests, Miss Jane Bennet and Miss Elizabeth Bennet. Georgiana invited them to come and be with her while William is away and will be here for two months.

How is it that Georgie has known Miss Elizabeth for so long and neither William nor I have ever met her? I believe she is a fit person to be Georgie's friend, but I cannot help but think William and I have been remiss in this. Have we been neglecting our duties? I feel uneasy that her legal guardians have been so lax.

To be sure, Georgie is excited about having the ladies here and I believe they will not take advantage of her good nature.

Your devoted son,
Richard

Having finished his letters, Richard prepared for bed and climbed between the sheets and was asleep in minutes. He had ridden hard all the way from London and such a journey is hard on the body and he was snoozing away before Georgiana and Elizabeth retired for the night.

When Elizabeth arrived in her room, Janice was there to help her get ready for bed. When all was done, she dismissed the girl and gathered the supplies to write her own letter to her father.

August 29,

Dear Papa,

Jane and I arrived at Pemberley today. The journey was long, but uneventful. The weather is fine, if a little cooler than at home.

Georgiana has planned for a number of activities to keep us busy for at least a week. There will be horseback riding, drawing and painting and tonight we indulged in playing the pianoforte and singing. Tomorrow we shall go to Lambton to see the town. I recall Aunt Gardiner was raised here and am eager to see the place.

I long to see the overlooks and the walking paths on these grounds. There is so much to see and do outside. Indeed, if I had the time I would inspect every inch of these grounds.

The grandest surprise was in the house. There is an immense library here with at least ten thousand books, if not more. You would love to see it, I am sure.

Please give my love to mother and my sisters.

Yours affectionately,
Elizabeth

When the letter was completely ready for the post, Elizabeth put it on the end table, blew out the candles and jumped into bed, pulled the covers to her chin and snuggled down for a long sleep. She slept soundly that night, with no snorers to interrupt her sleep or any crying babies to awaken her in the morning. For the first time in her life, Jane was awake before she was.

Janice came in to awaken her at eight in the morning and asked her if she would like a cup of chocolate. Elizabeth took the cup and sipped it all before stepping the first foot to the floor.

"Miss Elizabeth, I have pulled out your green muslin. Will that suit you this morning?"

"Yes, it will. Have you by any chance found the green grosgrain ribbon?"

"I have found it. Everything has been laid out for you."

"Thank you, Janice. Elizabeth went into the dressing room to wash up and put on her undergarments and Janice helped her into her gown. Sarah dressed her hair, and then Elizabeth dismissed the maid.

Elizabeth peeped into the sitting room but saw no one, so she stepped out into the hall, took her bearings and walked to the top of the stairs. She was starting to go down but turned when she heard someone call her name.

"Colonel Fitzwilliam, were you late this morning as was I?"

"I rather think I was. Riding from London on horseback wears a fellow out. May I escort you to the breakfast room?"

"Certainly you may, kind sir. I am famished."

The two walked down the stairs and then down two halls before entering the breakfast room. Jane and Georgiana were almost finished, but stayed behind until the others two had eaten. The Colonel decided to go for a ride when the ladies went to Georgiana's room to go through her riding habits. When she opened the door to the room and they went in to go directly to the closet door into the dressing room. Jane and Elizabeth were astonished to see their friend's extensive wardrobe. Her maid pulled out habit after habit, totaling an even dozen.

Georgiana selected one made from a burgundy wool fabric and handed it to Elizabeth. "Lizzy, this is one that is too small for me. It is only slightly out of style, so will you try it on to see if it needs to be altered in any way?"

The maid helped Elizabeth out of her gown and into the habit, which had a ruffled blouse and a snug fitting jacket. The skirt was voluminous, and a trifle too long. The maid took measurements and began to pin up the hem.

"Georgie, this is a lovely color. How does it look on me?"

"You look charming in it. There is a hat that goes with it, and it will frame your face beautifully." The hat was made in a mannish style with a broad brim and a high crown. A satin ribbon secured it under Elizabeth's chin. "Elizabeth, you may keep this habit, for I cannot wear it any more."

"If you insist, I shall keep it. I do love this color."

"Now, Jane, we must find one for you." Georgiana held up one and then the other and set aside the rejects. The maid took those away and put them back into the closet. "Jane, will you try this light blue one?"

Unfortunately, the light blue on was too tight, so Georgiana handed her a darker blue habit, which fit nicely. Nothing had to be done to it. The hat was found and given to Jane along with the habit.

"Thank you, Georgiana. I do appreciate your generosity."

"Do you think any of your sisters could wear the other two? I need to remove them from my closet."

"I think our Mary could wear the light blue one and Catherine the brown one. Lydia is too tall for any of them, but she does not ride at all, so has no need of one."

"Very well, Lizzy. I will have them sent express to your sisters. The maid will find the hats that go with them."

"I am sure the girls will receive these habits with pleasure," said Elizabeth.

Jane and Elizabeth finished dressing and the maid adjusted their hair.

"Shall I send a shawl to your sister Lydia? Shawls do not have a particular size, do they?"

"I believe they are all cut to the same size."

"We should get ready to go to Lambton. Shall we meet downstairs in fifteen minutes? I shall call for the carriage immediately."

They split up to go get their spencers and bonnets and then met down in the front entry hall at the appointed time. The carriage pulled up and a footman opened the door to allow the ladies to enter. They settled themselves, but before the carriage moved off, the door opened again and the Colonel asked if he could accompany them. Georgiana invited him into the carriage and when the door was again closed, they were finally moving on.

The ride to Lambton took a half an hour to arrive at their destination. The first errand to approach was for Georgiana to order a day gown. After choosing the fabric, style and trim, they left to go to the mercantile to look at ribbons. Elizabeth found a color she liked to replace one that had frayed and she also selected a pair of stockings. Jane purchased some new straps for her stays. Georgiana looked through the shawls and asked Elizabeth to choose one for Lydia. She chose one and all purchases were paid for. They then took a stroll down the street, Elizabeth walking with Georgiana, and Jane with the Colonel.

"Elizabeth, did you once mention to me that hour aunt live in Lambton as a girl?"

"Yes, I did say so. She left to marry my Uncle and they moved to London to be near his business. She was nineteen at the time and I have often wished to come and see her old home. She is such a kind lady, full of grace and good will for everyone."

"Perhaps you could bring her here for a reunion with her old friends some day in the future. Mrs. Reynolds told me she had met your aunt's mother. Her husband owned the sweet shop across the way. I believe her brother owns the shop now."

"May we go to the shop? I have not seen him in ages. He does not come to visit my aunt very often, at least not when I am in London. I would really love to see him."

Georgiana turned around and told the Colonel and Jane they would go to the sweet shop next. They ambled over to the shop and entered. A young woman was behind the counter arranging things. Georgiana asked, "Martha, is your father here?"

"Yes, Miss, he is in the back. I shall go and tell him you wish to see him."

"Tell him Miss Darcy wishes to see him for a moment."

The young woman hurried to the back of the store and returned promptly with her father.

Mr. Turner looked over those before him and said, "Miss Elizabeth Bennet, what brings you here to day?"

"My sister and I are visiting Miss Darcy for a couple of months."

"Mr. Turner, I would be pleased to invite you and your family to Pemberley for a picnic on some fine Saturday in October."

"Thank you, Miss Darcy, we would love you accept your invitation. Just let us know when you have decided on a date. Now, may I introduce you to my daughter, Martha?" Martha stepped forward and curtsied. "Martha, Jane and Elizabeth Bennet are your cousins by way of the marriage of my sister to their uncle. I think you already know Miss Darcy and her cousin Colonel Fitzwilliam."

"I am pleased to meet you cousins and to see you again Miss Darcy and Colonel Fitzwilliam."

"It is a pleasure to see you again, Miss Turner."

"We must be on our way now. I will be sure to send you a message about the day of the picnic as soon as I can arrange it."

"Before you go, would you care to choose some sweets to take home with you?"

"I for one would love to," said Elizabeth. "I have a craving for some of those lemon drops."

"Ah, you have chosen my sister's favorite. I shall prepare a box for you." Mr. Turner pulled a box from the shelf and filled it with lemon drops, enough to last at least a week. He closed it and tied a string around it and gave it to Elizabeth. "Miss Lizzy, I hope you enjoy these."

"Thank you, uncle. I know we will all enjoy them."

The party left the shop and walked over to the bookstore. "Georgie, thank you for allowing us to see our uncle. We rarely see my aunt's family and I consider it a special treat to do so now."

"I was my pleasure, Jane. There are members of my family that I rarely see, but they are not as nice as Mr. Turner."

"Are you thinking of Aunt Catherine, Georgie?"

"Yes, Richard, I am. She can be so embarrassing sometimes. She frightens me at other times."

"I suppose every family has embarrassing relations. Ours is our mother. She cannot control her tongue," said Elizabeth. "Our Aunt and Uncle Gardiner are very nice, though."

They stepped into the bookstore, where Elizabeth was in her element. She scanned the shelves with interest until she espied a new title and pulled it off the shelf. It was a small book describing the short-line railroad in Wales. She decided to purchase it and took it to be wrapped and to pay for it. The Colonel asked to read the book when Elizabeth was finished with it.

"I think we should go back home now. It is getting late."

Georgiana led the group out while the Colonel held the door open. He signaled Caleb to bring the carriage to them while they waited on the cobbled sidewalk. When the carriage pulled up, the Colonel handed the women in at which point Caleb pulled him aside and spoke quietly to him. The Colonel raised his brow and indicated he understood the man. He was quiet during the ride home and went straight to his room to write another message to his cousin.

August 30,

Darcy,

We were in Lambton today and Caleb said that some of the stable hands at the posting inn have seen Wickham in the area. I shall put the guards on alert and will tell the women to be extra vigilant when they are outside, and never go out without a guard or two."

Richard

He prepared the letter to be posted and wrote "urgent' across it and left the room to find the courier. He gave the message to the man along with a purse of coins to pay for his expenses to Ireland.

The ladies had gone to their rooms to refresh themselves, to come down a short time later. They found the Colonel pacing the floor. "Cousin Richard, what is the matter? You seem to be agitated about something."

"Please be seated and I will tell you." The women sat down and waited expectantly. "When we were in Lambton, Caleb discovered that Wickham has been sighted between here and Derby. We all need to be vigilant when we are out and about."

"Colonel Fitzwilliam, forewarned is forearmed. I for one will be especially observant," offered Elizabeth

"I was told you know about Wickham. If you spy him, get help immediately."

"Who is Mr. Wickham?" asked Jane.

Georgiana explained who he was and what he was capable of doing and Jane's eyes widened in dismay. "Would he try to harm one of us?"

"He is unpredictable at best and could very well try to harm you if he becomes agitated enough. Just stay together when you are out and about. There is safety in numbers. I have sent a message to William to let him know the man was spotted in the neighborhood."

Elizabeth took Jane's hand and squeezed it and did the same for Georgiana.

The Colonel concluded, "This news is worrying but I am sure the danger is not immediate. Just be careful."

"I think we should teach Jane and Georgie some defensive moves."

"What have you in mind, Miss Elizabeth."

"My father taught me some of the moves when I was attached several years ago. I was not harmed then because father interrupted the attacker and threw him off the property, but he taught me some defensive moves so I would be able to protect myself under any similar circumstance. Sometimes ladies can defend themselves if they know the right moves to take. Other times it is wise to be aggressive. Jane and Georgie are basically passive individuals, although I can see some outgoing traits in Georgie. I think it is reprehensible to keep women ignorant of ways to protect themselves."

"Not all men favor submissive women. We do not all want a doormat. I dare say you do not mean what you have said universally."

"Of course not, but in the case of Mr. Wickham it does, and to a great many other men in this country."

"If you wish, I can teach you ladies some tricks to use when in a difficult situation. We can, perhaps, use the ballroom for the lessons. There is plenty of room in there to move around freely. We can begin tomorrow. Will that do, Miss Elizabeth?"

"I hope so. I would not want any of us to be harmed in any way by this particular individual."

CHAPTER TWO

On Sunday morning everyone met after breakfast to go to the chapel at Lambton. The clergyman greeted them warmly and they took their seats in the Darcy family box while the residents of the town and the Pemberley servants took their seats in the rest of the pews. Elizabeth listened carefully to the sermon, based on the Gospel of Luke 18:18-30, about the rich young ruler who could not give up his riches to join Jesus and the disciples. She decided that money was a frivolous thing to base one's faith on. She believed her faith was a gift from God and she owed Him all that she had. After the service Georgiana spoke to some of the neighbors and introduced her guests to them.

When they went back to Pemberley, they had a light meal of sandwiches and tea and following that the women went to their rooms to don their riding habits. As they did that, four horses were being saddled in the stables and they were ready when everyone else was.

Georgiana had a dappled horse she named Polka Dot. A shiny black mare named Raven was fitted out for Jane, and for Elizabeth a much smaller animal named Chloe was fitted out. This horse was suitable for Elizabeth's small stature and lack of experience riding a horse. Colonel Fitzwilliam rode his usual brown stallion named Wellesley. Two guards also mounted their horses for they would follow the others on their ride.

They rode to a lookout point that was an hour's ride from the house. Elizabeth was charmed by the view, but Jane spent special attention on the colors of the trees in the valley and the mountains all around. This view gave her an idea for a painting. Had she thought about it she would have brought her sketchbook with her on the ride.

The habit Elizabeth wore looked better now that it had been hemmed up and she felt quite good in it. She knew it looked well on her for she was not blind to what she saw in the mirror when she put it on. Jane was all that was charming in her habit, and so was Georgiana, who wore a green one with a ruffled shirt and the hat was perched perkily on her head. The Colonel could not help be proud of his company, and he thought he had a good deal to speak to his cousin about when the man finally came back home.

The return ride took them to another location on the estate grounds. A meadow appeared before them, which was surrounded by fruit orchards. The apple trees were loaded with apples not quite ready for picking, but very close to it. On another side were walnut trees, and Elizabeth could see workers gathering the nuts and placing them in baskets.

They had been out for hours so they return to the stables and left the horses there and went inside the house to clean up and change clothes. The rest of Sunday was spent at leisure; everyone chose a favorite activity and quietly worked on them. Elizabeth was comfortable settled in the library reading, Jane was sewing on some handkerchiefs, and the Colonel played at billiards for while. Georgiana practiced on her pianoforte in the music room.

While Elizabeth was deep into her book on the railway in Wales, the Colonel walked in and sat down near her. He waited for her to recognize him and when she finished a paragraph, she looked up and said, "How can I help you, sir?"

"Miss Elizabeth, may I ask you something of a personal nature?"

"You may ask me anything but I reserve the right to refuse to answer if it is too personal."

"The thing is, I have been developing some feelings for you sister Jane. I would like to know if she is currently promised to another, and if not who do I speak to about asking to court her?"

"First of all, she is not promised to anyone at present, and of course you would have to speak to our father to gain permission to do so. She is of age and can make up her own mind, but contacting our father would be nice on your part. I do caution you to go slowly, for my sister has been crossed in love before and she is wary of other men's intentions."

"That man must have been a cad and stupid to let such a sweet lady go. I have noticed she is reserved and cautious, so I will try to go slowly. I have never felt this way about another woman and it is unnerving."

Elizabeth chuckled, "I wish you good luck and I may even ask her about her feelings for you."

"Thank you, Miss Elizabeth. Can you tell me about the other gentleman?"

"He came to Hertfordshire to lease an estate called Netherfield near us. Not long after he moved in he and his sisters and brother-in-law came to the assembly one night. They were introduced to my family and he asked my sister to dance and he spent some time with her at the assembly and asked her for the last dance. She was flattered by his attention that he gave her. Mother formed the intention of pushing my sister toward him and prophesied that she would marry him some day.

"His sisters thought my family was beneath them and urged him to stay away from us, but he did not listen to them. Our family has lived at Longbourn for four centuries and my father is a gentleman but the Bingley's families were tradesmen. The entire time he stayed at Netherfield he paid attention to my sister and led her on.

"Do not get me wrong. I have nothing against tradesmen, for my uncle Gardiner is one, but we must be sensible about who is above one and who is not. At any rate, Mr. Bingley held a ball in November and was still paying attention to my sister and she expected a proposal from him, but it did not occur. The next day he left for London and his family followed him and he let the lease lapse. My sister was heart broken because she had developed feelings for him."

"Are you speaking of Mr. Charles Bingley?"

"Yes, it is. Do you know him?"

"I do and so does my Cousin Darcy. Darcy met him when they were at Cambridge. Although he is an affable gentleman, he does fall in and out of love at an alarming rate. I dare say you and your sister do not often come to town. If you were familiar with what happens there, you and your sister would have known to be cautious when he came calling. He is not a bad man, just inconstant when it comes to women. He can also be persuaded to think he has made the wrong decision by the pressure of his sisters. Darcy tried to point him in the right direction but the is not always available to be of any assistance. The boy needs a keeper, one who is not one of his sisters. Some day I suppose he will grow up and become a real man."

"I admit my sister and I might be naïve in comparison to those who live in town, but we are not stupid. We do spend time in town once or twice a year, but we do not associate with those outside of our circle, except I do associate with Georgiana at her invitation. The closest we get to the ton is at the opera or the theatre."

"Are there no suitable gentlemen in your home town?

"No, the persistent war has taken those of the proper age, many who never come back. I am sure you know all about that sort of thing. Therefore we have a high share of spinsters who will take whomever is available. I for one will not marry anyone I cannot love and Jane feels the same. My mother is beside herself with five daughters and no sons, and she tried to make me marry Mr. Collins, our cousin and the heir of my father's estate. I refused and Papa supported my decision. She will never forgive me for my perfidy."

"I feel the same way that you do, Miss Elizabeth. I have found no one in town whom I would deign to give my heart to have it become broken because my wife had taken a lover."

"I pray that my sister and I will find what we want. And, you sir, are on the right track. I will let you know when I have spoken to my sister."

"Again, I thank you, Miss Elizabeth. This has been an enlightening talk." He rose and left the library to find Jane to sit with her. She was in the smaller sitting room sewing with Georgiana beside her, watching as Jane plied her needle.

"Good evening, ladies, what are you doing?"

"Jane is embroidering some handkerchiefs. She and Elizabeth have a special design they use. It is very intricate."

The Colonel peered at the design. "I have seen this design before. Is it part of your family crest?"

"It is, Colonel. The crest has been in the family for many generations. My father has a signet ring with the crest engraved on the jeweled inset."

"Can you draw the entire crest for me, Miss Bennet? It looks so familiar."

"I can draw it fairly well. Tomorrow when we prepared to draw and paint I will draw the crest for you."

Elizabeth entered the room and asked, "What will you draw, Jane?"

"I can draw the family crest. The Colonel said this design looks familiar to him and he would like to see what the whole crest looks like."

"Oh, I see. Do we have a time to get together to draw and paint, Georgiana?"

"We do, Elizabeth. Jane and I have decided to do it after breakfast and if it does not rain we will work outside on the east side of the house. We want to catch the morning sun to do our work."

The butler entered and announced that dinner was ready, so they all got up and trailed each other to the breakfast room. They continued to discuss the painting party during the meal, deciding what to paint or draw. After dinner they set up a card table and played cards until bedtime.

When they all went to their rooms, Elizabeth knocked on Jane's door and asked her if she could have a word with her. Jane let her in and they sat on the bed and Elizabeth brought up the subject of Colonel Fitzwilliam. "Jane, I had a discussion with the Colonel earlier and he would like to know what you think of him. He appears to be developing serious feelings about you but did not wish to frighten you with them. What do you think?"

"Lizzy, I think he is a fine gentleman and I like him a great deal. He is nothing like Mr. Bingley as far as I can see, and he has had a lot more experiences in the world than that other man. I think I would not mind getting to know him better. I am perhaps ready to reach out to him and develop serious feelings about him."

"Do not be surprised if he asks to court you. He did ask whom he must contact for permission. I told him to write to father, but that you are of age and you can make your own decisions."

"I am ready to make that decision should he ask me."

Elizabeth patted her hand and kissed her on the cheek. "I believe you two will be a good match if it comes to that. I will leave you ponder over this now. Good night, Jane."

"Good night, Lizzy."

The ladies dressed for bed and both spent time thinking about the situation. They fell asleep by midnight and Elizabeth slept soundly

When the Colonel came down to breakfast on Monday, the butler handed him a letter from his mother. He opened it and read it in the hall.

Richard,

To ease your mind, I must tell you that I have spoken to Darcy about the relationship between Georgiana and Miss Elizabeth Bennet. I have been in her presence a number of times, and I have met with her aunt twice. I can say wholeheartedly that she is a fine young lady and is a good example for Georgiana to emulate. Under her influence our Georgie has begun to come out of her shell and is not such a timid little thing any more,

Her sister Jane is a wonderful lady as well. Even though I have not met her, her aunt praises her for her accomplishments and her beauty. I cannot say the same about the two youngest girls, but they are young and with a little discipline may turn out well. I have met Mr. Bennet and Mr. Gardiner, their uncle.

51

By the way, neither you nor Darcy has been remiss in your duties. You may rest easy on that subject.

Your father sends his love as I do. Give my regard to the ladies.

Your mother,
M. Fitzwilliam

The Colonel refolded the letter, smiled, and placed it in his pocket. He walked into the breakfast room and greeted Elizabeth who was generally the first to come downstairs in the morning. "Miss Elizabeth, good morning. I have a hand a letter from my mother and she sends you her regards."

"Oh, I must write to her. I am remiss in my correspondence lately."

"Do you correspond with my mother regularly?"

"I write to her about once per month and have done so for a year. She likes to hear about my activities."

"Did she know about your trip here?"

"I thought Georgiana wrote to her to let her know what her plans were. I was sure she would not have sent the invitation if she had not alerted someone in the family. Did not your your mother send you to provide some supervision for us."

The Colonel laughed, "I think Georgie may have forgotten to do that.

"I am not sure what business Darcy has at his Irish estate. He raises horses there and he has a competent steward who manages it for him. To be called away so suddenly worries me, and then to have sightings of Wickham adds to my concerns."

"Allow me to show you something that I have to help protect Georgiana. My father insisted I keep one with me on the trip because he was worried about the length of the journey." She put her hand in her pocket and pulled out a lady's pistol.

"My word, Miss Elizabeth, do you know how to use that thing?"

"I do know how to use it. My father taught me to use it when I was seven and ten. I usually keep it safely put away it its case, but when you mentioned a cur would be around I thought I should arm myself. I plan not to let Georgiana out of my sight when we are out. My fear is that she would be his target for mischief."

"You must show me how you manage the pistol later. Put it away before your sister or my cousin come down. I am sure it would frighten them."

"Jane knows I can shoot, but she is unaware that I brought the pistol with me. I fear Jane is totally unprepared to protect herself in the event of an attack or any kind."

"Would you care to have another cup of tea?"

"Yes, please."

The Colonel stood to pour the tea and poured himself a cup of strong coffee. At this juncture he felt he needed it. Elizabeth was certainly an intrepid girl. He handed the tea to Elizabeth and just as he was about to sit down with his coffee, Jane and Georgiana arrived.

"Good morning ladies. Come and have a seat." The Colonel sat down and the ladies picked up a plate and filled them to their liking and sat down, Jane beside the Colonel and Georgiana beside Elizabeth.

Georgiana took a bite of toast and swallowed it with a sip of tea before saying, "Elizabeth I wish to begin a portrait of you. Would you mind letting your hair down and putting a ribbon around your head to hold it in place. I wish to note the length of the tresses and the natural wave that you have. My aim is to have you painting a portrait of my cousin while I paint you. I have smocks for us all to wear to keep our gowns clean while we paint and draw today."

"Georgie, do you expect me to sit that long?"

Elizabeth grinned, "You must at least sit long enough for me to catch your mood, the way the light affects the color of your clothing and your eyes. That should take but a few hours."

After breakfast everyone went to prepare for the morning activity. Elizabeth in particular had to call her maid to take down her hair and coax her hair to behave. The maid passed a thin ribbon around her head and tied it into a bow. Elizabeth dismissed the girl and grabbed the smock and put it on. She then picked up her sketchbook and pencils before joining the others on the east lawn.

Jane was already seated before an easel and was obviously sketching a portion of the house and its garden. Georgiana was arranging her materials on a table brought out by two footmen, who stood by to await further orders.

"Come, Elizabeth, sit here at this easel and Richard, you take the chair before her."

Elizabeth sat and opened her pencil case and pulled out one suitable for sketching her subject. She picked a knife and sharpened the pencil to her liking. "Colonel, could you turn to your left slightly?" He shifted to his left, and readjusted his sabre to a more comfortable position. Elizabeth began to draw, talking to the Colonel all along.

Georgiana's easel was positioned at an oblique angle so she could capture the pose she wanted of Elizabeth. She liked the way Elizabeth was interacting with the Colonel and she wished to capture the amusement in Elizabeth's expression.

The Colonel was surprised that he was having a good time sitting for his portrait. Never had he been so entertained by the quips being tossed around by the ladies. He could not see what Jane was doing but he could hear her quite clearly. He had not noticed that her sense of humor competed Elizabeth's so well, even if a bit more subtle.

The artists worked until the sun moved to another position and changed the shading of the subjects so Georgiana called a halt to the procedures. They all stood and stretched before begging to see all the canvases and drawing papers. The Colonel did not expect to see so much done on the portrait Elizabeth worked on. It was a half-length portrait showing the exact angle of the sword, the detail on the hasp, the buttons on his jacket and his medals.

Jane had drawn the garden and part of the house and Georgiana had drawn a good deal of Elizabeth's figure from an angle that showed her tresses and her profile. "We have made a good beginning so we shall meet here again tomorrow and Wednesday.

That afternoon the Colonel gave the ladies some lessons in defensive moves. Jane and Georgiana were embarrassed by some of them, but Elizabeth urged them on, saying it was important for them to know what to do in a crisis situation. They planned to meet again for three days to continue practicing these moves.

The art sessions continued through Wednesday as the girls moved from sketching to painting. Elizabeth and Georgiana chose oils to do their work and Jane chose watercolors. They made a good beginning on Wednesday, but had to move their equipment inside when it began to rain later that day.

The rain continued through Thursday and it rained so heavily and it was so dark, no painting could be done inside. There was not much they could do, but the arrival of some letters cheered them considerably. There was one for the Colonel, one for Elizabeth, and one for Jane.

The Colonel opened his and read,

September 1

Richard,

I will be leaving Ireland tomorrow. I have handled the problem here and since I am concerned about the Wickham sightings, I shall take the first ship out. Keep a watch over Georgie and the other ladies.
I have known that Georgiana and Miss Elizabeth Bennet had been corresponding but I have not been able to find the time to meet the lady. I am looking forward to being able to do so soon. I should be home by the seventh.
Are you engaged to one of the ladies yet?

F. Darcy

The Colonel smiled and then let Georgiana know when her brother expected to be home, weather permitting.

"What good news, Richard. I can scarcely wait to introduce him to the Misses Bennet."

Jane opened her letter from her father and read,

September 2

My dear Jane,

You cannot imagine my surprise when I received a message from none other than Colonel Richard Fitzwilliam, the son of the Earl of Matlock. What truly surprised me is that he has asked for permission and my blessing to court you. Have you really agreed to do so?

All funning aside, I do give both of you my blessing. He seems to really care for you and I hope you feel the same for him. I am eager to meet your beau, but I imagine you would want to wait until you come back home. Give the fellow the attached note from me.

How are you and Lizzy getting along with Georgiana Darcy? What is Derbyshire like and how is the weather there? Your mother wants to know everything.

Your loving father,
T. Bennet

Surprised at what she read, Jane took the letter and note to the Colonel. "Sir, I see you wrote to my father about a courtship, but I do not recall that you had asked me for one."

"I wrote to ask him if I might ask you, and if I did, would I have his blessing. So it appears he has given it, and now I do wish to ask you if you will permit it."

Jane thought a moment, "Colonel, I will permit it for I do wish to get to know you much better."

The Colonel smiled broadly and took Jane's hand and kissed it. "You say he sent me a note as well."

Jane handed him the note and he read it. "Let us go tell the others now." He slipped the note into his pocket and the two of them walked over to Elizabeth and Georgiana.

"Elizabeth, Georgiana, we have an announcement to make. I have a note from Mr. Bennet and he has given Miss Bennet and me permission to court her."

Georgiana jumped up and hugged her cousin and in turn hugged Jane. Elizabeth put down her letter from her Aunt Gardiner and did the same. Elizabeth whispered in her sister's ear, "I knew this would happen." Aloud she said, "I am confident you both will be happy."

Georgiana called for some wine to toast the couple.

CHAPTER THREE

Friday the rain began to diminish but it was still too wet to go out to paint, so the easels were set up in the ballroom after a tarp was placed on the floor to protect it from dripping paint. Elizabeth covered her canvas with a thin coat of white paint to create a uniform surface to apply the rest of the paint. When it was set enough, she began to sketch the figure lightly over the white paint. Bringing it to the point where she could apply color, she mixed the paints to her specifications and began to paint in earnest. After working for close to four hours she was ready to quit for the rest of the day. The light was dimming and making it difficult to get things the way she wanted them. Therefore, she cleaned her brushes and covered the palette. The others appeared ready to stop to have tea also.

Georgiana had done much the same as Elizabeth, but Jane, using a different medium, used her own system. Those two were ready for the tea so they cleaned their brushes and put them aside for the next day.

They cleaned themselves up, had their tea and prepared to do whatever they wanted for the rest of the day. Elizabeth was ready to get some exercise, so she told Georgiana that she would be out side for a while. Georgiana would practice on the pianoforte for a while and Jane said she would rest for a while.

Elizabeth asked Caleb and Jacob to accompany her on her walk. The men followed behind Elizabeth as she led them to the woods on her walk. She had noticed on the previous night that there had been smoke issuing from among the trees and she thought that was suspicious, so she wanted to investigate the matter. When they entered the woods, she asked the men if they could smell anything out of place. They all sniffed and detected the remains of a fire. Caleb went one way and Jacob and Elizabeth went the other way. It was not too long before Elizabeth and Jacob came to clearing that had obviously been used to light a campfire. Now Jacob knew Mr. Darcy did not allow anyone to camp so close to the house, so he called for Caleb to come and help in investigating the area.

He picked up a stick and stirred it through the ashes, and move around some leaves and found a spent whiskey bottle. There were also traces of a meal or two.

"Miss Bennet, it appears someone has been scoping out the house and that does not look good. Let us go to back to the house and speak to the Colonel about this."

"I had suspected something like this."

Caleb asked his brother, "Shall I alert the others, Jacob?"

"Yes, you do that while I speak to the Colonel. We need to protect the ladies so speak to all the men on the estate. You and I will stay near the ladies, but the others are to scan the area for anything that looks suspicious."

Jacob and Elizabeth hurried back to the house and found the Colonel in the billiard room. Jacob explained what they found and the Colonel took Jacob to the study to talk strategy for protecting everyone. They were enclosed in the study for an hour before Jacob was released to do his assigned job.

The Colonel thought it would not hurt to write to his father and ask his advice so he quickly penned a letter and sent it by courier. He then went to the ladies to speak to them. "When Elizabeth went for a walk, she and the men found a campfire in the woods. This is evidence that someone had been watching the house and the activities of us all. For one thing, no one is allowed on Pemberly grounds to camp, and certainly not so close to the house. Therefore, we must be on high alert. No one is to go outside unless she has a guard or two with her; we will keep all the doors and windows locked until the situation is resolved. I have given instructions to Mrs. Reynolds and her husband to instruct those under her purview to be vigilant and let us know if anyone they do not know comes lurking around.

Jane and Georgiana showed signs of dismay and nervousness. "I will not be able to sleep tonight, Lizzy. Will you spend the night with me in my room?"

"Certainly, I will, Georgiana. I would not mind at all. Jane, how about you?"

"I will lock my door and the door to my dressing room and the sitting room door."

"We shall do the same in Georgie's room."

"I doubt Wickham will be able to get into the house with all the guards moving around and about."

"Colonel, there is no harm in trying to feel secure by locking all the inner doors. Jane is probably not the target anyway."

"If it makes you feel better, Georgie, I can sleep in your sitting room."

"Cousin Richard, I would, indeed, feel safer if you did that. I can have a maid bring up some blankets and pillows for you. For the rest of the day, we should all stay together."

That night Elizabeth brought her nightgown and robe to Georgiana's room and changed in her dressing room. When both were ready for bed, Georgiana locked the dressing room door and the door to the hall. The Colonel had been given the pillows and blankets, and he took off his jacket and waistcoat, and pulled off his boots, made up the settee and discovered it was much too short for him. He decided to make up his bed on the floor. It had to be more comfortable than the settee. It was not long before he was fully asleep.

In the wee hours of the morning, at a time when all should have been sleeping, Elizabeth was awakened by a noise in the dressing room. No one should be there at that time of the morning, so she awakened Georgiana and told her to get under the bed, which she did quickly. Elizabeth put on her robe and pulled the pistol out of her pocket, she aimed it toward the dressing room door, and when it opened as she had suspected it would, she said, "Take one more step and you are a dead man." She heard the person take two more steps, so she pulled the trigger and fell backward from the report of the gun as she heard the intruder fall and hit his head on the dresser.

The Colonel was startled awake and he grabbed his sword and barged into the bedchamber. Running feet were heard pounding down the corridor and Jacob entered the room with a lantern in his hand. He handed it to the Colonel who took a look at the intruder. "He is out cold. Go find some rope so we can tie him up and send for the doctor and the magistrate in Derby. Miss Elizabeth, are you all right?"

"I will be in a few days. The gun's action pushed me to the floor."

"Where is Georgie?"

"I am under the bed. Can I come out now?"

"Yes, Georgie, you can come out. It is safe now," said Elizabeth.

Georgiana climbed out from under the bed, her hair in disarray and with cobwebs strung about. "The maids should dust under there," she said and sneezed.

"Are you well, Georgie?"

"I am fine, how about you, Lizzy?"

" I will do, Georgie."

Elizabeth stood up cautiously, having collected a few bruises in her nether regions.

The Colonel turned Wickham over to see where he had been shot and noted it looked like a superficial wound. His major problem was the bump on his head. When the servant came back with the rope, Wickham was tied up and taken to the hospital room on the ground floor. Guards were stationed inside and outside of the room. The Colonel told the women to go to the Elizabeth's room and clean up and wait for him to call for them. He then called the Reynolds couple to begin questioning the staff. Someone had to let Wickham in and he suspected it was a staff member.

Georgiana and Elizabeth cleaned up and changed into day clothes rather than staying in their nightgowns. The day was getting brighter and neither one thought she could go back to sleep under the circumstances, so they took seats in Elizabeth's sitting room. They ordered some tea and toast and it was delivered in good time. Elizabeth decided to check on Jane and found she was still sound asleep. She had not heard the report of the gunshot and slept right through it.

She rejoined Georgiana who asked, "Now what do we do?"

"I suppose we wait for the Colonel to call for us. There is not much more we can do, is there?"

A maid brought the tea and toast and some jam as well as two apples for them. They ate as much as they could manage on nervous stomachs and waited. It was around nine in the morning when Elizabeth had enough of waiting and she was ready to scream in vexation at the apparent delay when the sitting room door opened to show before them the man in the painting in the gallery hall. Elizabeth gaped and Georgiana jumped up and almost knocked the poor man down. "Oh, William, you have come. Have they told you what happened?"

"Yes, Poppet. Our cousin told me the whole story. Now, is this your friend Miss Elizabeth Bennet?"

"Brother, she is he heroine of the day. She saved me from Wickham. It is Elizabeth. Elizabeth, this is my brother William."

"It is a pleasure to finally meet you, sir."

"And it is my pleasure to finally be introduced to you. We bumped into each other the bookstore in London, did we not?"

"We did sir, and I remember it."

"My cousin said I owe you much for using your quick wit on trying to solve the situation here. Thank you most heartily. Now tell me, are you well?"

"Brother, she woke me and told me to crawl under the bed when Wickham unlocked the dressing room door. She told him to stop and if he took one more step she would shoot him, and she did. Then he fell and bumped his head, and she fell backward. I do not know where she had the pistol but I am happy that she did."

Elizabeth blushed and looked down. "Georgie, it was a gun my father gave to me when I was attacked by a bad man. My father taught me to use it safely and I have had since I was seven and ten. It has been in my pocket since we learned that Wickham was seen in the area."

"Brother, can we come out now? We have been in here since three this morning and I know Elizabeth is about to run off to get some exercise."

"I think so, Poppet. Come on down to the sitting room. You will find your aunt and uncle down there for Richard sent for them. I will go with you and your friend."

He offered one arm to his sister and the other to Elizabeth, but he noticed Elizabeth was a little shaken. "Miss Bennet, I think you are a little upset."

"I dare say I am sir. I have never shot anyone before and it is unnerving at best. It is quite different than when one is shooting at targets."

"The doctor said the wound is superficial, but he did bump his head and that knocked him out."

She held on to his arm and felt the comfort he offered. They went down the sitting room where Lord and Lady Matlock awaited them. Lady Matlock stood to grab Georgiana by the hand and sat her down beside her on the settee. Mr. Darcy led Elizabeth to a seat and eased her into it.

"Tell me, girls, are you quite well?"

"I believe I am, but Elizabeth is a little shaken, aunt."

"I dare say she is. Did you really shoot the man, Elizabeth?"

"I did, my lady. He did not stop when I told him to, so I pulled the trigger. I would not allow him to harm Georgiana for the world. Have they found out who let him into the house?"

Mr. Darcy answered, "Everyone is being questioned by the magistrate from Derby."

The Colonel entered the room and asked Elizabeth if she needed to see the doctor before he left. Lady Matlock said, "Yes, she does. She is quite shocked by the incident and may be in need of a composer."

The Colonel helped Elizabeth from her chair and took her to another sitting room where the doctor awaited for her. Her lady's maid was there as well. "Doctor, this is Elizabeth Bennet. My mother thinks she may be in need of a composer."

"Allow me to check over her and see how she is. It will only take a short time." The Colonel left and the doctor talked to Elizabeth about her ordeal. He checked her heart rate and her pulse then asked her if she were in any pain.

"Yes, sir. I fell backward when I pulled the trigger and landed on the floor. I dare say I will feel bruises by tomorrow."

"Allow me to see your hands." He looked at her hands and discovered some burns from the powder from the gun. "As I expected you have some powder burns. I can treat them and they will heal quickly." He called for some water and towels and he cleaned the wounds and applied some salve, then wrapped her hand. "Your maid should change the bandage twice per day for at least three days. That should do the trick for the hand and any bruises will heal on their own. I will leave you with this herb to put in hot water or tea before you go to bed. It will help you sleep. If you need me for anything else, just send me a message and I will come as soon as I am able. You did what you had to do to protect Miss Darcy and yourself."

"I dare say I did, but I wish it could have been otherwise. I thank you, sir. I appreciate your help today."

"I think everyone is happy that you had the wit and sense to be prepared for any eventuality. There is no shame in that."

"No sir, I think you may be correct."

"Now, allow me to take you back to the sitting room." He held his hand and she put her left hand in his and rose. He offered her his arm and walked her to the sitting room, opened the door and led her in to help her to sit down.

"Mr. Darcy, Miss Elizabeth has been given instructions and I am confident she will follow them explicitly. She will be fine in a day or two. If you need anything else in the future, please feel free to call on me. I shall be going now."

Mr. Darcy walked him to the door and asked about Wickham's condition. "He will be well enough to go to his trial in a few days, but I must say he should be locked up and the key thrown away for frightening two innocent young ladies. It is a shame the bullet did not go two inches more to the left."

Mr. Darcy chuckled, "Good day doctor and thank you." He watched the man as he left then went to find the Colonel, who was still in the infirmary hall.

"Well, Darcy, you came just in time. Did the rain hold you back any?"

"It did hold me back by half a day, or I would have been home last night. I am sorry that poor lady had to go through such trauma in my home. She will probably form a distaste for the place."

"I think not, man. She loves the library and the walks out side. I think she feels at home here."

"I hope so."

"Now, what was the problem in Ireland?"

"The usual tenant dispute that happens from time to time. They would not listen to my steward, but I was able to solve the problem with a little common sense. I am just sorry I was not here when all of this started."

"I hardly think you would have done anything different. Were it not for Miss Elizabeth's suspicions about some smoke in the west woods, we would not have found the campsite that Wickham used to spy on us. This put the men on high alert, so we had guards inside and out. Miss Elizabeth was prepared for she has been carrying that little pistol in her pocket for days."

"Do you think Wickham could have crossed her path in the past. She did say a man attacked her when she was younger, which was when her father bought the gun and taught her to use it. He insisted she bring it with her on the trip here."

"No, it was nothing like that. She simply has a high regard for Georgiana and she said she would protect your sister with her life. My mother said she has always been that way since the two of them met."

"To think that in the year or so that Georgie has known her I had not been introduced to her until now. I have seen the lady in town on numerous occasions with an older couple and I even bumped into her in the bookstore. She always seems to be happy with her life and the things she is doing."

"Elizabeth told me she met Georgiana in Lambton when she was traveling with her uncle and aunt. My mother met her at the Alesbury tea and she was astonished at the way Georgiana blossomed under the Elizabeth's attention to her. Elizabeth and Georgiana have been corresponding and meeting one another from time to time in town."

"Is there anything you need to tell me? I noticed you have called both ladies by their first names."

"Miss Jane Bennet and I are courting. I said I would choose one of them for myself, and I meant it. I received the blessing from her father yesterday. I have saved Elizabeth for you, for she is more you type."

"So where is the beautiful blonde?"

"She slept through the whole ordeal. Since the staff has been under investigation all morning, no one has been up to help her. I believe mother went up a little while ago to rescue her. She could not understand what was happening for no one answered her call on the bells. Jane and I have since had a comfortable chat."

The men went back to the sitting room and Jane was down with the others. Elizabeth was there, trying to hide her bandaged hand from her sister.

"Lizzy, I see you are trying to hide your hand. What did you do to it?"

"It is just a little powder burn. It will be better by next week. I had to shoot at Wickham to keep him from coming all the way into the chamber."

"Do you mean you really shot him?"

"Yes I did. It was only a superficial wound, but he fell and bumped his head on the dresser, which knocked him out. He was out long enough for the Colonel to tie him up and take him to the infirmary room. The magistrate from Derby has been questioning the staff all morning to discover who let him in."

Someone must have been able to begin work in the kitchen for a laden tea tray was brought in and placed on the tea table. There were sandwiches, tarts, and biscuits to feed an army. Full tea and coffee pots were ready to be poured. Richard offered to get some tea for Jane and Mr. Darcy offered to get one for Elizabeth. Georgiana followed behind her brother and prepared a plate for Elizabeth and one for herself. The brother and sister took the items to Elizabeth and they put them on the side table next her chair.

Jane looked at her sister and said, "Elizabeth, I believe I know only half the story. Can we meet some time today and talk about it?"

"Perhaps some time this afternoon we can meet in the library. I am all talked out now and I have yet to see the magistrate."

"Do you think I should write to Papa?"

"I will take care of that in the morning. By then I can tell him the whole story. You know he would want that from me."

"What surprises me is that you brought that thing with you."

"Papa insisted I bring it. He does not trust these long trips to be safe for young women traveling alone. Had I left it at home, either Georgiana or I could have been injured in some way. You know I would fight in that circumstance."

"I suppose I do know it, Lizzy." Jane thought back to the time Elizabeth was attacked. She screamed and fought the man until Mr. Bennet arrived to assist her. He kicked the man out and threatened to call the constable if the man ever set foot on Longbourn property again.

"I say, is anyone going to introduce me to the charming young lady?" bellowed Lord Matlock.

"I am sorry, father. I should have done so when I came in. Father, this is Jane Bennet, Elizabeth's elder sister. Jane, this is my father, Lord Henry Fitzwilliam, Earl of Matlock."

"It is my pleasure to meet the young lady who has caught the eye of my son. He told me he is courting you."

"Yes, sir, he is. My father sent his blessings and we received it yesterday."

"If you are anything like your sister Elizabeth, I think I have nothing to say against the match, should matters come to that."

"Thank you, my Lord, but I must say there is no one who could compare favorably with my sister," said Jane.

Elizabeth smiled and shook her head.

"Jane, I think you are all that is perfect for me. I like you just the way you are," said the Colonel.

A knock on the door heralded the presence of Mrs. Reynolds who announced that the magistrate would like to speak to Miss Elizabeth if she is free to come to him. Elizabeth stood up, took a deep breath and walked over to Mrs. Reynolds and then followed her to the library where the magistrate was conducting his interviews. She was announced and the magistrate waved her a chair without looking up. When he look up he was astonished to see the petite little woman sitting before him. He noticed her bandaged hand and guessed the cause of the injury.

"Now, Miss Bennet, can you relate to me the details of what occurred this morning?"

"May I begin with the day before, for I believe what was discovered then is pertinent to the issue."

"Please go ahead, then."

She explained she noticed smoke issuing from the woods the night before and that she had two of the guards to go with her on the next day to investigate. They found a fresh campsite there and the guards alerted all the men on the estate and they told the Colonel. They believed that Wickham had been watching our activities. That night they all decided to lock up the house and even all the inside doors, which they did. Georgiana did not wish to sleep alone, so Elizabeth related that she stayed with Georgiana that night and the Colonel made up a bed in his cousin's sitting room. Very early in the morning Elizabeth related that she heard a noise coming from the dressing room, so she told Georgiana to get under the bed, and that she put on her robe and pulled the gun from the pocket. When Wickham opened the door, she told to stop or she would shoot him.

"He stepped further into the room and I warned him, so I pulled the trigger. I dare say he was surprised, but he fell forward and hit his head. The colonel immediately came in and one of the guards was right behind him with a lantern. No one really believed Wickham would get into the house, but he did anyway."

"Miss Bennet, I have but one more question. How is it that you had the pistol in the first place?"

"My father insisted I bring it with me. He taught me to use it after an attack on my person when I was younger. He wanted to see that I was protected in the future and he has been concerned about by continued safety. I started to carry it in my pocket when I first heard that Wickham had been sighted in the area. I would protect my friend with my life if I had to. With all of the guards around here I cannot fathom how he managed to get into the house."

"All will come out in due time, Miss Bennet. You may go now."

Elizabeth left the library and went back to the sitting room. Georgiana was called in next and she looked beseechingly at her brother who walked her to the library and stayed in the hall until she came back out. All she had to do was tell what she remembered of the incident and she told it as honestly as she could. She left the library and her brother asked, "How did it go, Georgie?"

"It went better than I expected. I just told him what I knew about this situation and about the last time we had problems with Wickham."

"Very good, my dear, I am very proud of you."

He walked her back to the sitting room and returned to the library to speak to the magistrate. "Sir, will his take much longer?"

"No, Mr. Darcy. I believe I have all that I need to determine what to do next. I shall charge the man with illegal trespassing, lighting a campfire in an inhabited area, and attempted kidnapping with the intent to do bodily harm. I cannot charge in with breaking and entering for someone let him.

"Might I use some of your men to transport the cur to the gaol in Derby?"

"I can provide you with the men you need. Is there anything else I need to know?"

"There is one more thing I can tell you. The one to allow him entry is one of your scullery maids. If I were you I would see that she is sent away. She seems to have no loyalty to you."

"I will surely send her away, but I suppose she must stay here to be a witness at Wickham's trial."

"Keep an eye on her, Mr. Darcy. She will need to testify. It may be that others will need to testify as well, so you may wish to warn your sister and the young lady that they may be called on by the courts. I think it is too bad the bullet did not go two inches more to the left."

"The doctor said the same thing, but I would not wish that on Miss Bennet. She is traumatized enough from this situation, but she felt she was protecting my sister."

"Indeed she was, sir."

The magistrate gathered his papers and put them in his satchel and left to arrange transportation of the prisoner.

Mr. Darcy returned to the rest of the party in the sitting room. "I believe we will have the house to ourselves in a very short time. The magistrate is now arranging to take the prisoner to Derby. He will be charged with attempted kidnapping and a couple of other pertinent things."

It was midafternoon before the magistrate had everything all arranged and he left leaving a sense of quietness in the house. The young scullery maid was brought into Mr. Darcy and she was in there for close to an hour, Mrs. Reynolds with her. Mr. Darcy had arranged for the girl to go to Ireland after the trial. In the meantime she would continue to work as a scullery maid at Pemberly, but under strict supervision. She was to receive no visitors, and she was not to set foot above stairs for any reason. This seemed harsh to Elizabeth but she understood the reason behind it. The results of the girl's misdeed could have had serious repercussions for the household.

In the sitting room, Lady Matlock was urging Elizabeth and Georgiana to go to bed and get some sleep because they had been up for so long. "Aunt, I cannot go into my room right now. It needs to be cleaned up before I step foot in it again."

"Come with me to my room, Georgie."

"Very well, Lizzy, I will take a nap with you."

Jane walked with the two girls as they went upstairs and saw that they were comfortably in bed before leaving them to their slumbers. The two had disrobed down to their shifts and climbed into the bed, and covered themselves with the blanket. Georgiana went to sleep quickly but Elizabeth lay their thinking of what had happened. She was unsure that she had done the right thing, but seeing the girl sleeping peacefully beside her, decided it was for the best after all. At length her eyes grew heavy and she slipped into a dreamless slumber.

They slept for four hours and awoke in time to dress before the sun went down. Elizabeth rang for her maid, who helped arrange the girls' hair and button their gowns. When they were ready to go downstairs, they grabbed hands and left the bedchamber. They arrived at the sitting room still holding hands.

Mr. Darcy and Lord Matlock stood and Mr. Darcy asked if the ladies had slept well.

"We did, Mr. Darcy."

"And now we are hungry, brother. When will we be having dinner?"

"It will not be ready for another hour and an half. The kitchen got off to a slow start after all that happened this morning. Shall we order some tea and sandwiches?"

"Yes, please, I could eat a horse."

"They sat down and Mr. Darcy called for a servant and he told the servant to order the snacks. Jane came up and sat by Elizabeth, "I hate to pry, Lizzy, but how is your hand?"

"It stings a little but it is not uncomfortable. Do not worry, it will be better in a day or two."

"Have you ever had powder burns before when you doing target practice?"

"No, I have not. I usually wear leather gloves when I practice."

Since Elizabeth had been seated, Mr. Darcy had not taken his eyes off her. The Earl, too, was looking at her curiously to see her reactions when anyone spoke to her.

"Lizzy?"

"Yes, Georgie."

"Will you feel well enough to go into Lambton tomorrow? I wish to purchase some new paints. I need them to finish my painting of you."

"I am sure I will be just fine tomorrow. I need some carnelian read as well."

"Have you all been painting?" asked Lady Matlock.

"We have, Aunt Margaret. Jane paints scenery and Elizabeth and I paint portraits. We had been working on the drawings for a few days and now have started painting. When it started to rain we brought everything inside and put it in the ballroom. Everything is still there."

"May we see what you have done so far?"

"After we have had our tea, we would be honored to show you our work."

The tray arrived and those who wanted anything partook of the tea and sandwiches. When they were sated each of them decided to join those going into the ballroom. Richard offered his arm to Jane and Lord Matlock took his wife and Georgiana, leaving Mr. Darcy to take care of Elizabeth, which he did willingly.

The evening sun lit the ballroom adequately for viewing the works. Jane's watercolor was dry up to the point it had been completed. The oils would take longer to dry but now they were still tacky to the touch. Lord and Lady Matlock looked with interest at the drawing of Colonel Fitzwilliam and then at the unfinished painting. They could see that Elizabeth had captured the Colonel's impertinent grin. "My dear Elizabeth, what do you plan to do with the finished painting?"

"I had made no plans for it. If you would like, I could have it framed and send it to you, My Lady."

"Indeed, I would love to have it."

"I am planning to prepare a kit kat of that pose to give to Jane."

Richard stood back to watch the others to admire the works, but he was especially interested in seeing his cousin's look when he saw the portrait Georgiana was doing of

Elizabeth. At the moment Mr. Darcy was looking at Jane's watercolor landscape and he told her it was very nice. He then went to his sister's work and stared at the drawing with is mouth agape. "Georgie, you have captured so much of the beauty of your subject. It will be a fine painting when you are done."

Elizabeth blushed when she heard what he had said and turned around to respond to Lady Matlock's request to see her sketchbook, which was lying on the tarp on the floor next to the easel. Elizabeth handed the book to the lady and she and her husband looked through it with interest.

"Among the sketches there are pictures of several young ladies. Who might they be?"

"They are my sisters, my lady. This one here is Mary, who is a year and a half younger that I am and the two other are Catherine and Lydia. Those two are twins, as you can see, and they are five and ten."

Mr. Darcy came up to see the book when the Matlock's were finished with it. They took their time looking at the sketches until they reached the last, which was that of a house. "Where is this, Miss Elizabeth?"

"That is one of the tenant houses on my father's estate."

"It appears rather large to be a tenant house, does it not?"

"I dare say you might say so, but it was on a piece of property my father purchased about five years ago. The steward lives there now."

"How large is Longbourn?"

"There are about three thousand acres, ten tenant houses, and the manor house. The manor house is modest by some standards but it has rooms enough for our large family and for any guests who come to stay with us. Five hundred acres are devoted to raising cattle and the rest is used for planting acreage. The income is more than adequate to sustain our needs and for my father to invest some each year. Even I have been able to invest some of my pin money since I was old enough to receive it."

"Lizzy, I thought you said you could not draw landscapes. This picture belies that statement."

"Georgie, perhaps I should qualify that statement a little. What I meant to say is that Jane is much better at it than I am. Hers are more artistic while mine are more architectural or graphic."

"There is something to be said for realism in drawing buildings," said Mr. Darcy. "I see nothing in this picture that is not artistic."

"I dare say the old saying is true then. Beauty is in the eye of he beholder."

"Indeed it is, Miss Bennet," said Mr. Darcy, as he looked straight at her. She handed the book to him so he could begin at the beginning.

Later, as they were all filing out of the ballroom, Mr. Darcy held his sister back and said, "Georgie, what do you plan to do with your painting?"

"I had thought to have it framed."

"If you do, may I hang it in my study?"

"If you wish I will see that it is done." Georgiana smiled up at him and then looked at Elizabeth who was walking out with Lady Matlock. She said nothing more, but her mind was churning with possibilities and delightful thoughts. She actually did a little skip out into the hall. Having Elizabeth as a sister was her fondest hope.

"You seem to be happy, Georgie."

"Oh, I am, bother. You are home and my best friend is here. Nothing could be better." Her brother laughed and patted her on the shoulder.

Mrs. Reynolds approached the group as they gathered in the hall, announced that dinner was ready, so the all moved on to the dining room. They took seats as they wished around the table, and Lord Matlock took the top of he table and the rest of them took seats to the right and left of him. Georgiana was on one side of Elizabeth and Mr. Darcy on the other. Lady Matlock sat to the right of her husband and Colonel Fitzwilliam beside her with Jane on his other side.

The meal was a lively affair with the Colonel and Mr. Darcy trading insults and other quips across the table, keeping the others laughing at them. Elizabeth and Georgiana planned what they would need to purchase on the shopping trip tomorrow. Jane kept up a conversation with the Lady Matlock, leaning over the Colonel to speak to him and occasionally to Lord Matlock.

Every so often, Mr. Darcy offered to cut a piece of food for Elizabeth since her hand was bandaged. She thought she could handle the task well herself, but she rather like being tended to in that way by the gentleman beside her.

After dinner the ladies left the men to their port and met in the music room. Elizabeth excused herself to go and write to her father and her Aunt Gardiner.

September 7,
8:00 PM

My dearest Papa,

Very early this morning I was obliged to use my little toy in earnest. Conditions required I do so, although I was unhappy at having to use it. A very bad man tried to attack dear Georgiana. I felt I had to protect her. The story is a longer one and I will tell it to you when I see you again. Rest assured that matters are under control now, the bad man was taken to gaol and will most certainly be sentenced severely. He is a little the worse for the ball in his chest and the bump on his head.

Do not worry about me. I fell backward from the report but have only received a few uncomfortable bruises which will take care of themselves in time and of course a few powder burns. Lord and Lady Matlock are here, as well as their son Colonel Fitzwilliam and Georgiana's brother, who arrived this morning to take charge of the situation.

The most amusing part of the whole thing is that Jane slept through it all, never even hearing the report from the pistol. She awoke late and could not understand why no one would answer her summons for assistance in getting dressed. At length Lady Matlock went up to help her and explain the delay.

All my love,
Elizabeth

The next letter was a little shorter for her hand was becoming itchy.

September 7

Dear Aunt,

Should rumors begin to fly about some unusual activity happening at Pemberly, be not alarmed. All is well as I write this evening and should go well from this day forward. To be succinct, a man tried to attack Georgiana, but I was with her at the time and was able to forestall the attack. He is now incarcerated in Derby to await his trial. I am well and Georgiana is well.

I suppose Jane will write soon with special information of her own.

We have been painting and drawing all week here at Pemberly and I wish to ramble all over and see what there is to see.

My love to uncle and the children,
E. Bennet.

Having finished the letters she called her maid to come and change the bandage before going back downstairs. Her hand felt better after the change and looked better as well. It would not take long for the burns to heal for they were not deep ones. She was also feeling much better about the whole affair and was ready to put it behind her.

She slipped quietly into the music room to listen to the music provided by Georgiana and she looked at all those who were present and smiled. She felt so at home with them and her surroundings. One member noticed her entry into the room and sudden smile she exhibited and wondered what had pleased her so.

He rose and took a seat near her and asked, "Miss Elizabeth, what brings you so much pleasure this evening that you smile so sweetly?"

"I was thinking how comfortable I feel in everyone's presence here. They all make my heart swell with love and joy. Everyone here is so dear to me."

"Everyone?"

She looked in him the eye and said seriously, "Yes, everyone."

"Miss Elizabeth, would it be possible for you to show me where you found the campsite in the west wood tomorrow?"

"I dare say I will have time in the afternoon for we ladies are going to Lambton in the morning to replenish our painting supplies."

"The afternoon will be suitable. I have some business matters to attend to in the morning." He thought for a moment. "Do you find your accommodations comfortable here?"

"Oh, yes, I do. I have been quite comfortable. Your servants are always attentive and kind to me. When we first arrived here both Jane and I were intimidated by the size of the this house, but once we became quite settled I find it is cozy and has so pleasant an atmosphere that I have found only in my aunt's home. Your sister has made us feel at home here."

"I am happy to hear you have been comfortable, but it grieves me you had to bear what happed this morning. We discovered the man was let in by one of my scullery maids. He managed to get through the guards defenses by dressing as a woman. Colonel Fitzwilliam has already spoken the guards about that."

"My hope is that we may all put this episode behind us, at least after the trial is over. I know I will have to speak about it to my father and to my uncle and aunt, but I wish to end it there. I have written some terse accounts to send to them and I am sure they will not be satisfied with it. Do not be surprised if one or the other makes an appearance in the near future."

"Any one of them will be welcome here at any time. Do not be concerned that I would even think of turning them away."

"Thank you, you have put my mind at ease."

"Lady Matlock came up and asked Elizabeth and Mr. Darcy to join the others to participate in a discussion that had been brought up by her son. They arose from their seats and followed her to those congregated in the center of the room. They took the available seats and settled into them.

"We have been discussing whether or not to go to London when Richard must report back to his duties. He is concerned his departure would disrupt his courtship of Jane and he does not want her to think he has abandoned her."

"What do the rest of you think of this plan?" asked Mr. Darcy.

"I am agreeable," answered Jane. "What about you Elizabeth?"

"I am Georgiana's guest and if she wishes to go I will follow."

"Then let us say it is settled. We shall plan to go by the end of September. Since things have been fairly well settled here, my wife and I will go back to Matlock and then meet you in town by the first of October. For now I am ready to retire for the night. Will you come with me, my dear?"

"Allow me to put away my sewing and I will accompany you." Lord Matlock waited for his wife and then they went on to their rooms hand-in-hand.

Georgiana then brought up another topic that had been bothering her. "Brother, I do not wish to sleep in my apartment tonight. Would it be possible to have another prepared for me and have my things transferred from one to the other?"

"I can understand why you would wish to do so, but it cannot be done right now. Where would you like to sleep tonight?"

"If Elizabeth does not mind I would like to stay with her."

"Have you discussed the matter with her?"

"Lizzy, do you mind?"

Elizabeth laughed, "I do not mind at all. I have often had one of my sisters spend the night with me. You can order some of your clothes to be brought in before we retire tonight."

Georgiana jumped up and tried to hug Elizabeth while she was still in her chair, almost knocking her over. "Hold on, Georgie, you are going to tip me over." Jane and Richard were laughing and Mr. Darcy held fast to the back of Elizabeth's chair. It was not long before they were all laughing at Georgiana's remorse.

Elizabeth stood and took her friend's hand, "Come, dear, we have things to do ere we go to sleep tonight."

"Do you need my help, Lizzy?"

"If you are offering, Jane, we could use you."

"I will send two maids to you, Georgie. Do not overwork the ladies."

Leaving the men behind, the ladies left to complete their self-appointed task and Mr. Darcy ordered that two maids be sent to assist them. He then took a seat next to Richard.

"Richard, what do you think about the situation we find ourselves in?"

"As you know, we had word several days ago that Wickham was in the area. As a precaution I alerted the men on the estate to keep a watch out for him. What irritates me most is that Wickham got through our defenses so easily. I ask myself what would have happened if Miss Elizabeth decided not to sleep with Georgie last night and did not have her pistol with her. I truly did not believe he could get into the house."

"I cannot blame you Richard. Wickham has always been a slick and slippery individual. He has fooled many a maiden lady. We cannot dwell on might-have-beens, but more on what did occur. I am concerned about Miss

Elizabeth. She wants to push the memory inside, but I do not think that is wise."

"I have seen many a soldier be devastated by having to shoot someone and others do not feel it so deeply. Miss Elizabeth had never shot an individual before, but she only inflicted a superficial wound. What she did was to delay the possibility of harm by, in effect, alerting me and the servants stationed in the hall. I was nearby and on my feet in seconds after the report and Caleb came running in carrying lantern to light my way. The fact that Wickham managed to hit his head is immaterial, for help was instantaneous. The servants and I had him subdued in no time at all."

"We need to make her understand that soon. I think being a heroine is not something she cherishes."

"Perhaps she does not, but tell me, what does she cherish?"

"All of us."

"Now that is interesting. You know, she was very well impressed by your portrait in the gallery."

Mr. Darcy turned a shade of pink and said, "How did you decide to court her sister?"

"I must say I was somewhat taken by both of them. Miss Elizabeth is every bit as beautiful as her sister, but her personality is vastly different. Jane needs someone to take care of her and that is what I want to do. Miss Elizabeth, on the other hand, can take care of herself. Another thing is that she is more intelligent that I am. Jane looks up to me, but Miss Elizabeth is far above me. She is more your type intellectually and you do favor brunettes, do you not?"

"I will confess something to you Richard that I have not told another soul. When I bumped into Miss Elizabeth in the bookstore, it was not the first time I have ever seen her. I had seen her with an older couple many times as they attended one event or another. I never had an opportunity to approach them for an introduction. Then I bumped into her at the bookstore. She said in her beautiful way, 'Excuse me.' I helped her pick up her purchases and she smiled at me and I was hooked by her lovely eyes."

"Man, I think you should declare your interest before it is too late and some other gentleman sweeps her off her feet."

"I will give it some thought."

CHAPTER FOUR

The women had the maids take a number of Georgiana's gowns, undergarments, stockings, and shawls to Elizabeth's room and placed much of it in the dresser drawers that were unused at that time. The gowns and shawls went in the closet and shoes were placed on the floor. There was plenty of room for everything for Elizabeth had only what she brought with her from Longbourn. By the time they were finished it was time to get ready for bed. Jane left to go her chamber and Elizabeth and Georgiana helped each other to undress and put on their nightgowns. Elizabeth had put on a pair of well-worn slippers.

"Lizzy, I think I shall purchase a new pair of slippers for you. Those on your feet are in tatters."

"I can buy my own slippers. You do not have to do that."

"I want to give you a gift and I want you to know I have decided to adopt you as my sister. Sister's give each other gifts, do they not?"

"I dare say they do, sister. You may buy the slippers but I shall buy the paint you need."

"Agreed," said Georgiana, smiling broadly.

They climbed into bed and pulled up the covers to their chins. Elizabeth leaned over to blow out the last candle. "Good night, sister."

"Good night, sister."

Both of them slept through the night, Georgiana much longer that Elizabeth, though. In the morning Elizabeth quietly slipped from the bed and softly walked to the dressing room. Her maid was there pouring water from a can into a washbowl. Elizabeth washed up and the maid helped her into her day gown and combed and styled her hair and then changed her bandage. Elizabeth tiptoed out of the chamber and into the hall and down the stairs to the breakfast room where she met the Colonel and Mr. Darcy.

"Good morning, gentlemen. It is a lovely day, is it not?"

"Yes indeed, and it just got lovelier when you walked in," said the Colonel.

"I expect it will be just as lovely this afternoon."

Elizabeth smiled and said, "I hope so, Mr. Darcy, especially if one wishes to go out rambling in the woods." Elizabeth went to the sideboard to fill her plate and when she was finished the footman carried a cup of chocolate to her seat. She settled into her seat and she bowed her head and said a quiet little prayer before picking up her fork.

While she had been praying, Lord Matlock entered the room and Elizabeth greeted him after she lifted up her head.

"Miss Elizabeth, are you always an early riser?"

"I am, my Lord, and have been since my youth. It was the only time of day I could be with my father when there were no interruptions. We took that time to go over my lessons from the day before and sometimes just talk."

"So your father taught you your lessons. Did you not have a governess?"

"No, my lord. My mother could not see the sense in them, much to the detriment of my younger sisters. I always thought they needed one, but mother would not allow it. My father taught me like a boy so now I am more intelligent than the rest of my family because I learned so much. Should I have children I would want a governess for them."

"So your sisters were not taught by your father?"

"I taught my younger sisters to read and do math, but they were not interested in learning more, except for Mary who was interested in learning about religion and philosophy, so my father taught her some of that and the rest she has taught herself. Jane is somewhat more educated than the rest of my sisters for she is the eldest of us. She was interested in certain subjects but I was hungry for more than that. I read on any subject I can get my hands on and my thirst for knowledge in insatiable."

"Miss Elizabeth?"

"Yes Mr. Darcy."

"Have any of your sisters been endowed with your quick wits."

"I suppose Catherine has, but it would be more useful if she were better educated. Perhaps all is not lost for I might be able to change her interests some day."

"Miss Elizabeth, I know you play the pianoforte quite well. Do any of your sisters play as well?"

"Colonel, Jane can play a little. She simply needs more practice time. It is difficult to get the time when there are three eager pairs of hands to one instrument for Mary plays as well. Catherine can play the violin quite well but Lydia has no interest in anything but ribbons and lace. You would think twins would be more like each other but Catherine and Lydia are vastly different."

"You have no brothers, I understand."

"That is correct, my lord. My parents have not been so blessed. My mother was disappointed when I was not born a boy and she has never forgiven me for the offense ever since."

"Is there an entail on the estate?"

"No, sir there is not. It was broken when my father was born. I do not know why there was before that. It is a family story I have not been privy to."

"So I gather one of your siblings or you is the heiress?"

98

"I dare say you are right but I have no knowledge of which one of us it is."

Elizabeth turned back to her breakfast and Jane and Georgiana joined the rest of them. "You must have awakened quite early. I did not hear you leave the room."

"Georgie, I awoke at my usual time and did not wish to disturb you, so I was as quiet as a mouse."

Mr. Darcy excused himself to go to his study to work on his correspondence and some business matters. The earl rose next to check on his wife, who was having breakfast in bed. The Colonel refilled his plate and offered to fill one for Jane. He did so and the footman brought her a cup tea. Georgiana was left to fill her own plate, but she did not mind at all. She cheerfully sat beside Elizabeth who was sipping on another cup of chocolate.

"Jane, will you go shopping with us today?"

"Yes, Miss Georgiana, I do wish to go. I need some more watercolors to finish my landscape."

"We shall leave after we finish here. I shall order to have the carriage brought around in a few minutes. Will that suit you?"

"That sounds fine. I would simply need to fetch my pelisse, bonnet and my reticule."

"I need to speak to my brother about our planned picnic with Mr. Turner and his family. We should do it before we go to London."

"We should plan to do so the week before our departure. It gives you time to plan and talk to your brother."

"Yes, you have a good plan, Lizzy. Is my brother in his study?"

"He is, Poppet, but he is conducting business this morning and you know he does not like to be interrupted when he conducts business. Perhaps you should wait until later today."

"We cannot tell Mr. Turner the time today, but we will tell him to save the Saturday before our departure. It cannot be done any later."

Jane and Georgiana finished their meals and all three women rushed to fetch their pelisses and other paraphernalia. The carriage was waiting for them when they came back downstairs. The Colonel followed them out of the dining room to meet his mother coming down the stairs.

"I understand the girls are going to Lambton. Will you go with them?"

"I had thought to go, but I think it may be better for them to go alone. They have not had much opportunity to do something together like that. They should be safe enough with Caleb and Jacob following them in horseback."

"Very well, Richard. Your father and I will go back to Matlock two days from now. Your father has some business to attend to before we go to London. And if you learn that Fitzwilliam has popped the question, I want to be the first to know."

"Mother, you certainly are a wise one. The man has already lost his heart and he just has to convince his mind. He has been carrying a torch for her for at least a year."

"How could that be? As far as I know they were not introduced to one another until yesterday."

"He has seen her in town on occasion but never was able to approach her to even speak to her except for the time they bumped into each other at the book store. Can you imagine his response when he discovered her in that sitting room holding Georgiana's hand after the incident? He knew Miss Bennet was friends with his sister but never knew she was the lady in the bookstore.

In the study Mr. Darcy was far from attending to business for he was leaning back in his chair, his hands clasped behind his head. He was thinking of he curly headed brunette bowling down the avenue with his sister. Now that he had finally been introduced he knew she was the one for him, but how could he make her understand what he wanted?

The lady in the carriage was listening to her sister and Georgiana but her inner thoughts were on a different subject. For the life of her she could not get the image of Mr. Darcy out of her mind. It felt so right to be at Pemberly, walking the paths of his home, doing things with his sister, talking to him about inconsequential things. She had never felt so at home and so treasured, not even at Longbourn. She felt she belonged at Pemberly but she knew it was nonsense, it could never be.

They arrived in Lambton and went into the shops, purchased their paints and slippers for Elizabeth and then went to the Sweet Shop to speak to Mr. Turner. He greeted them warmly and asked about their welfare having heard about the incident at Pemberly.

"We are all well and the invader has been taken to Derby to stand trial. None of us were harmed although we were threatened. Now everything is as it should be."

"I am happy to hear this. If my sister writes I will tell her all is well."

"I have written to her as well and I told her if she heard of any rumors that they were probably exaggerations and to just ignore them. All is well, indeed. Jane has written to her with some interesting news of her own. Shall you tell him Jane?"

"I do not see why not. It is no secret and I do have father's permission. Uncle, Colonel Fitzwilliam and I are courting. His mother and father seem to be happy for us and I could not be more pleased."

"Mr. Turner, I wish to reiterate my invitation for the picnic. It will be on the third Saturday of this month, but I will get to you later on the time as I have to check with my brother on that."

"I shall mark that date on my calendar. My family is eager to attend."

"We must be going now. Give our regards to your family."

"Good day, ladies. We look forward to seeing you at the picnic."

The carriage pulled up and they all entered and began to discuss when they would paint again. It was then that Jane remembered she should have drawn her father's crescent. "Lizzy, I forgot all about drawing the family crescent. I feel so silly."

"It is not too late to do so. Start it when we arrive back at the house. I am sure it will not take you too long."

"Surely there is no rush to complete it. We have to finish our other works and I think you are very close to completion on your watercolor."

"I do owe the Colonel an apology, though, for I as much as promised I would draw it."

"I am sure he will forgive you. A lot has been going on and it is no wonder you forgot," said Elizabeth.

"Lizzy, do you think we can finish our oil paintings before we go to London?"

"If we work diligently we should be able to do so. If we want them ready by Christmas they will have plenty of time to dry. And we should be able to get them framed."

"I cannot decide what color frame to use. How do you decide on the matter?"

"I choose a color that would complement the painting. What color do you wish to bring out in it?"

"I want to emphasize your hair color."

"Then you should select some mahogany colored stain for the frame."

The carriage pulled up in front of the portico and the Colonel and Mr. Darcy were out front waiting. Both of them assisted the ladies to disembark. "Was your trip to Lambton a success?"

"It was brother. We all found what we wanted and made a visit to the Sweet Shop to speak to Mr. Turner. Did you know he is related to Jane and Lizzy by marriage? His sister is married to their uncle."

"No, I did not know that. Was the sister raised in Lambton?"

"Yes Mr. Darcy, she was here for her first seventeen years. Jane and I stay with the Gardiners when we are in London. They are our favorite members of the family. When we are in town they take us to the theatre or the opera or other events."

"I believe I have seen you with them on occasion, Miss Elizabeth."

"You may have done so, for I go nowhere with anyone else. I believe your aunt knows Mrs. Gardiner well."

"Miss Elizabeth, my aunt knows many people, and loves only a few. I think she loves you."

"I am very fond of her. You must understand, that my aunt and uncle to not encroach on circles above their own, but they do get invited to dinners once or twice a year by people in the upper circles."

"Where do you and Jane fall in he level of social circles?"

"Sir, our father is a gentleman, but my mother is the daughter of a solicitor. My uncle is an importer and exporter of exotic and rare goods."

A gust of wind blue a cinder in Elizabeth's eye, so she took a handkerchief out of her pocket and tried to remove it. With little effort it came out when she wiped the tear from her eye. She blinked and dabbed again.

"Miss Elizabeth, are you all right?"

"I simply had a cinder in my eye. It is fine now."

Mr. Darcy notice the design on the handkerchief and said, "What is that design on your handkerchief?"

"Sir, it the scroll works on our family crest. Jane and I often embroider the scroll on our handkerchiefs."

"I was supposed to draw the full crest for Richard, but completely forgot to do so. If you wish to have a drawing, I will do it today."

"That is quite all right, Miss Bennet. I think I can find what I need in the family archives. Take a look at my ring."

Elizabeth and Jane looked at the ring. "It is very much like Papa's ring, except for the lower right quadrant."

"How long has the ring been in the family?"

"I believe Papa said it has been around since 1765. It belonged to his father and his grandfather before that. His great great grandfather's name was Henry D'Arcy-Benét. His great grandfather changed the name to Bennet."

"The Darcy family is a branch of the D'Arcy family. So were the D'Arcy-Benéts."

"How interesting. I must write to Papa and let him know what you have said, I am sure he would want to know."

They reached the front door and the butler opened it to let them in. The ladies took their purchases to their rooms and left the bonnets and pelisses there. They joined the others in the drawing room where the Matlocks were. Mr. Darcy and the Colonel were explaining the relationship between the two families and this discussion lasted through tea and scones. When tea was over the party began to break up, Jane and the Colonel going with Georgiana to the music room, Lord Matlock to the library and Lady Matlock to check on the progress of the work being done in the new apartments chosen for Georgiana.

"Miss Bennet, this looks like a good time to go and see the campsite. Are you quite ready to do so?"

Elizabeth went up to retrieve her bonnet and pelisse and the two of them took their walk to the West Woods. They left from the garden door facing the woods and Elizabeth led the way to the campsite; her hand was nestled on his arm. As they continued their walk Mr. Darcy began to express his feelings for her.

"Miss Elizabeth, do you remember the day we bumped into each other at the bookstore in London?"

"I remember it quite well. You were so apologetic and I must say quite tongue-tied."

"To be honest with you, I was astonished that I had come so close to the most beautiful woman I had ever seen. I am not a man who can speak with a silvery tongue as others do, but what I say is heartfelt."

"Since we are being honest and open, I have often thought of that day and wondered who you were. It is true I had seen you in company on occasion, but never knew you were Georgie's brother. When I saw your portrait in the gallery I was stunned,"

"I hoped that one day we would meet again. You are everything I imagined you to be; kind, loving, witty, and intelligent."

Elizabeth blushed, "And you say you do not have a silvery tongue. I beg to differ."

They turned to the right and shortly came upon the camp sight. Mr. Darcy looked around. "Miss Elizabeth, what I have to say now may shock you, but I have a notion that it would help to wipe the memory of Wickham from your mind. " He turned and looked her in the eye. "Will you marry me?"

"Indeed, I am shocked, sir. I was not expecting this from you."

"Surely I was not supposing you would be expecting a proposal from me. If you need time to consider the matter you may have it. My rationale is that I have known you in my heart for more than a year and had hoped it might be true of you. You are more than I could ever have dreamed you to be."

"Perhaps I have always carried an image of you in my heart, and perhaps that image is what I see before me. From your sister I have received nothing but good reports of you and even if I make allowances for a certain bias on her part, I can scarcely believe any of it was exaggeration. What can I say to your proposal but a resounding yes, I will marry you? And another thing we could do to erase the memory of Mr. Wickham is to plant azaleas and rhododendrons in this location and before that is done I think you have the responsibility to explain all this to my father."

"It would be my pleasure. Now before we go back to the house, may I kiss you?"

"You may, sir." He took her in his arms and tipped her chin up and kissed her warmly. He stepped away and she said, "That was lovely."

"Come, my love, we must be getting back before Richard sends out a search party."

The couple walked out of the woods, hand in hand, to meet a couple of the guards earnestly looking about them. "Gentlemen, you may go about your business. Miss Elizabeth and I are quite well and need no assistance. If one of you would go and find my gardener and send him to me, I would appreciate it."

The guards turned on the spot and went in search of the gardener, leaving the couple to amble back to the house. Colonel Fitzwilliam greeted them in the foyer. "Where did the two of you lope off to?" We missed you and I sent the guards out to find you."

"There was no need to find us, Richard, for Miss Elizabeth was merely showing me the campsite. She thinks we ought to plant rhododendrons and azaleas in there to erase some unpleasant memories."

"Did you say "we" ought to plant them? Who is "we'?"

"My future wife and I will see them planted."

"Do you mean that you have asked Miss Elizabeth to marry you already? You work fast, do you not?"

"It has taken me a year to get close enough to ask her."

"Mother will be pleased, to say the least. Let us go in and tell her."

"We were headed in that direction, Richard, and would like to continue with our walk back to the house. You must know we should write to her father for permission."

"That is a minor detail. I cannot imagine any father refusing you permission. Come, the others are in the drawing room waiting for word of you and discussing plans for going back to London."

At the drawing room door, the Colonel barged in and announced joyously, "Ladies and gentlemen, I believe Fitzwilliam has an interesting announcement to make to you!"

Mr. Darcy bowed, "This day it is my pleasure to announce to you that Miss Elizabeth has accepted my pleas to be my wife."

Jaws dropped and it took several moments before Jane rushed up to her sister and hugged her. "This is quite a surprise, Elizabeth, but yet, I am happy for you."

"Thank you, Jane. I am happy as well."

Lord and Lady Matlock and Georgiana then came up and expressed their joy at the news. Lady Matlock had always thought the two of them would do well together if they ever had the chance to meet. It had been her desire to see him well settled with someone his intellectual equal.

Georgiana was especially delighted at finding Elizabeth would soon be the sister she always wanted. She hugged Elizabeth tightly and then she hugged her brother and thanked him for proposing to her dear friend. He laughed and kissed his sister on the cheek.

Lord Matlock offered his support, "Congratulations, my boy. You have secured a real treasure. You may count on my support."

"Thank you, uncle, I appreciate it."

"Fitzwilliam, I knew in my heart this day would come, but not so soon."

"This charming lady has been on my mind since I first saw her in London with her aunt and uncle time and time again. My mind was settled when we bumped into each other at the bookstore one day. And then to see she was the one who had befriended my sister and was sitting there in the sitting room of her chambers the two of them holding hands to comfort each other. I wanted to hold her and help her forget about what happened earlier that morning, but propriety would not allow it. I now must write to her father and explain myself to him. She is afraid he will not understand."

"'You, William, may be deficient when speaking but you do quite well when explaining things in writing. I think her father will not be too hard on you. Should he need to speak to one of us, we could be willing to help him understand. Fell free to write us at Matlock," explained his Lordship.

"I had better get to it. It will not do for rumors to precede my explanation. If you will all excuse me, I shall be in my study." He left to go to his study and begin his compelling rationale.

After he left the others settled Elizabeth in a chair and urged her to tell them how the proposal occurred. She told of his request for her to show him the campsite and they made arrangements the day before to go there on this day. She said it was there he asked her to be his wife and give her some better memories of the site, so she suggested planting the bushes there. She did not go into any detail of who said what, for that was something she would keep in her heart and her heart alone.

"Do you wish to marry in Hertfordshire or in London?"

"My Lady, we have not discussed matters that far yet. We must determine whether or not to have a long or short engagement, and large or small wedding, or where to hold it."

"Tell us your preference. I am sure it would be important for him to know what is on your mind. If I know him he would like a minimal of fuss connected with it."

"To be honest, I would prefer a smaller wedding to a larger one with family present but few others."

"So you like things to be simple?"

"I do, the simpler the better suits me fine. What would bother me is if my mother gets involved in the planning. She would ignore my wishes and plan it the way she thinks it should be. Perhaps it would be better to have the ceremony in London, and then maybe I could order things as I would like them to be."

"Should you need my assistance in any way I offer it to you wholeheartedly. I will not interfere unless you invite me to do so. I remember when I was married; my mother went over every detail six or seven times and it drove me to distraction."

"Should my mother be involved, I will be driven mad with her interference."

"Jane, what do you say about planning a double wedding," barked the Colonel.

"You have not proposed, so I do not know."

"I am proposing now, will you be my wife?"

"I rather think I will."

"Well, well, what more can we expect today?" asked His Lordship.

"I do not know, but it seems I have a letter to write to Mr. Bennet as well. Excuse me while I try to compose a convincing letter to the man."

He went to Mr. Darcy's study and knocked on the door and when Mr. Darcy responded to the summons, he opened the door. "Darcy, old chap, I too need to write a letter to Mr. Bennet. Can you give me what I need to do the job?"

"What is this? Have you proposed to Miss Bennet?"

"I did, but probably in a less romantic way than you no doubt did."

"I do not know how romantic it was, but my Elizabeth seemed to be pleased with my approach."

"We were all sitting there discussing your wedding when it came to me there was no reason to wait to propose to Jane so I did. Now we can have double wedding and save on expenses."

"So you had an audience when you proposed?"

"I did, so I cannot back out now. Give me some paper and pen and let me get on with my task."

In the sitting room, Elizabeth excused herself to write a letter to her father, hoping to soften the blow.

Three days later Mr. Bennet received three express letters from Pemberly. He had just managed to digest the letter from Elizabeth about the incident two days before and was quite surprised to get mail from her, Mr. Darcy, and the Colonel. To be honest, he was not surprised that Jane and the Colonel had come to an understanding, but the one from his favorite daughter and Mr. Darcy astonished him. He read those letters again and put down his spectacles and called for Mr. Hill.

"Mr. Hill, pack my trunks for I will be making a journey to Derbyshire as soon as it is packed. Have my carriage made ready."

"Yes, sir, right away sir."

Next, Mr. Bennet called for his wife and when she entered he announced, "Mrs. Bennet, I shall be going away on some important business. While I am gone, the girls are to stay at home. I do not wish to hear of them getting into trouble while I am gone."

"But what is so important that you have to leave so suddenly?"

"First of all, Jane has agreed to marry this Colonel Fitzwilliam she was been courting for, say, about a week. Now I have two messages telling me Elizabeth has accepted a proposal from none other that Fitzwilliam Darcy. And this other bit of news has me completely baffled. I shall go and clear everything all up."

"You certainly will not interfere with the engagements, will you? You must know this is the best news I have had in years."

"I knew you would think that way, and it is true it would not do to have the engagements broken now for the scandal would be tremendous. Of course, Jane is of age and Elizabeth is nearly so, therefore they ought to know their own minds in these affairs. But I certainly want to meet these men before I offer them my blessings."

"Why can we not all go?"

"That would most likely do more to damage to the relationships than anything I could say. You and the girls will stay here and pay mind to your own affairs and stay out of those of the two eldest girls. Do I make myself clear? There will be no gossiping about the engagements and no exaggerations about their prospects."

"Oh, Mr. Bennet, you do try to vex me!"

"With these letters came the packages for the girls from Miss Darcy. See that they are properly distributed."

Mrs. Bennet took the packages to the sitting room and called for Mary, Kitty and Lydia to come to receive them. Each girl was given a package and Mary opened hers and exclaimed, "This is exquisite. I have never had anything so fine."

"Look at mine, Mary. It is just what I needed," said Kitty.

"And see what she sent me. This is the softest shawl I have ever owned. We all must write and thank her for everything."

Mary and Kitty ran to their rooms to try on the habit and hats and Lydia pranced around the room so show off her new shawl to her mother and Mrs. Hill, who was there to carry away the wrappings. Mrs. Bennet could not wait to run to her sister Philips house to brag about the gifts to her daughters and, of course, she could not resist announcing the engagements.

Three days later Mr. Bennet arrived at Pemberly and stunned the whole party there. The Matlocks had already gone to Matlock so they were not around to be stunned.

"Will somebody tell me what kind of den of iniquity is being held here?"

"Father, it is no such thing," answered Jane.

Colonel Fitzwilliam stood out in his military best, "Mr. Bennet, I presume? If you would give us but a few moments to settle down, we will answer all of your questions in a civilized manner. Shall we repair to the drawing room?"

Everyone settled into chairs and Mr. Bennet asked, "Which of you is Mr. Darcy?"

Mr. Darcy stood, 'It is I, sir. How can I help you?"

Mr. Bennet looked up at the imposing gentleman before him. It was not so much the man's height that gave Mr. Bennet pause, but his bearing that impressed him most. "Sir, I have come to discuss the letter you sent me. How long have you known my daughter Elizabeth?"

"I have known of her for more than a year and have seen her in town on occasion over that period when she was out with, I presume, her aunt and uncle. She was always outgoing and lovely on those occasions and I believe she entered my heart at the time we bumped into each other at the bookstore last year. Since then I have done my best to be introduced to her but to no avail. Can you imagine my surprise when I discovered she was the same lady who had befriended my dear sister, and to see them together here at my home sealed my desire to make Miss Elizabeth my wife."

"So you choose a wife by seeing her on occasion but never speaking to her. Is that not unusual?"

"It may be, sir, but all I can say now is I love her with all of my heart and do not wish to live without her."

"Do you feel the same about him, Elizabeth?"

"Father, I know you are teasing us now and I do not appreciate in the least. Without a doubt, I do love him and have since the incident in the bookstore. You have always said I could choose who I want to marry and I chose Fitzwilliam. All we need is your blessing."

"Well, it seems you mean to have each other, so I do give you my blessings. You and your Colonel also have my blessings, Jane. All I need from you know is the settlement papers, and the sooner the better. Now, Mr. Darcy, about this other matter, I need a clear explanation of what you mean by it?"

"I believe I can explain it best by showing you some documents describing the split between our families. If you will follow me I can ease your mind quickly. Georgie, will you have a maid bring a tea tray to the library for Mr. Bennet and me?"

Georgiana ordered the tray for her brother and one for the rest of them as well. The somewhat dazed party in the drawing room took their teacups and sipped a supporting amount of the brew before relaxing.

"Jane, is your father always like that?"

"No, not always, but you must know Elizabeth is his favorite daughter and he is more concerned about her welfare than he is about the rest of us. Indeed, Elizabeth is equal to him in intelligence and quickness of mind so it is no wonder he favors her company to those of us who speak of nothing but ribbons and lace. He will say he has not heard a sensible word since we left Longbourn."

"Life will not be the same for him, then."

"No, it will not, with both of us planning to leave home at the same time. But I am sure we will invite him to stay with one of us from time to time to give him some respite."

"You may be sure Papa will always be welcome wherever I am, Jane. Remember, he has yet to explore William's library. I would wager that he will not be paying so much attention to what William is saying now since he is in there."

The butler then entered the room and handed Jane and Elizabeth some letters that had just arrived. Elizabeth had a couple of more missives than Jane.

"Do you two mind if we read these here? They are from family and friends who I dare say have heard about the engagements," asked Jane.

"We do not mind at all, my dear. Georgiana and I can keep each other company while you read."

The girls from Longbourn sent their congratulations and there were letters from their mother filled with unneeded advice on the practice of keeping their betrotheds interested until the weddings. Elizabeth had one from her friend Charlotte and she wondered how her friend learned of the engagements so quickly. Apparently her mother had already been around the neighborhood telling everyone of their good fortune.

Elizabeth's last letter was from her Aunt Gardiner who had heard from her brother that his family had been invited to a picnic at Pemberley on the following Friday. She wrote to wish them well and hoped they would have a good time.

Her aunt had also received the letter that Elizabeth sent about the engagements and she offered Elizabeth and Jane housing while they were in town.

The last letter was from Mrs. Philips who also knew about the engagements. It was obvious to Elizabeth her mother had been very busy on that day.

"Jane, I have a letter from Aunt Philips and one from Charlotte. Everyone in town now knows of our engagements."

"I have one from Susan Ames. I suppose mother could not keep the news to herself, could she?"

"Why is it a problem for everyone to know that you two are engaged?" asked Georgiana.

"Our mother will exaggerate the news beyond recognition. She will tell everyone she had everything to do with getting us together and encouraging us to find husbands while we were away, and that is not why we came here. It was to be with you and have a good time. Finding husbands was unexpected and surprising to us. We will not have a moment's peace from her from now until the weddings are over. I have every intention of staying in London for the whole engagement period. I wish to be married in William's parish and I want to have control of my own wedding."

"I do as well, Lizzy. You know how mother can talk me into to choosing what I really do not want."

"Do not worry about that, Jane. My mother will do all that is possible to keep your mother out of your way while you make plans. Did she not say so before she left for Matlock?"

"She did, Richard, and I will rely on her help."

"Aunt Gardiner offered us housing while we are in town, if you were concerned about that, Jane."

The Colonel was called into the library to join Mr. Bennet and Mr. Darcy and the women began to plan in earnest for their weddings. Georgiana pulled out a notebook and pencil to take notes and the two prospective brides made known their wishes.

"Since we are listing all that we want, we can enlist the aid of Lady Matlock and our aunt to do the necessary shopping. We shall choose what we want before Mama comes to town so we will have all the say we want when choosing our gowns and bonnets.

"Georgie, will you stand up with me?"

"I would be delighted and honored, Elizabeth."

"I shall ask Mary to stand up with me."

"Good, Jane. We have that settled."

"I would like my wedding gown to be of a light blue silk with seed pearls embroidered at the neckline, short sleeves and elbow length gloves. My bonnet shall not have feathers on it and only a bit of lace to encircle the crown. My slippers will match the gown. Have you got all that, Miss Georgiana?"

"I do, Miss Bennet. Now, Elizabeth, what do you want?"

"I would like an overlay of palest sheer sea green silk over a gown of white silk. The bodice will be of the white silk also and so will the slippers. I will have no trim at the neckline, but will wear my pearl necklace instead. I want three-quarter length sleeves and wrist-length gloves. On my head I want a veil of the sheer sea green silk."

"You both have chosen colors that will look well together as you go down the aisle. I will choose a light green so as not to clash with your gowns."

"I believe we have a good plan of action. We only have to wonder what mother will choose for Mary. Perhaps we could tell Mary of our plans and she could insist on something suitable for her own gown."

The men all came trooping back to the drawing room and took seats as they found them. "Well, Papa, is everything as it should be?"

"Lizzy, it has turned out well, I should say. Apparently you and Mr. Darcy are reuniting a family that has been at odds for a couple of centuries. Since this is the case I did well in choosing the heiress to the estate. Elizabeth I have named to be the next owner of the estate and I ask that you leave it to your second born son, should you have one, if not your second born daughter."

"I am astonished, Papa. I was certain you would want to leave in to Jane."

"It had been in the past left to the second eldest son. For a few generations that practice was not followed. I thought it incumbent upon myself to reinstate the practice now."

"I suppose there is some logic in there somewhere but right now it escapes me entirely."

"Jane will receive an inheritance of fifteen thousand pounds in addition to one thousand pounds that she will receive upon the demise of you mother. She is not being shortchanged in any way. Neither will the other girls, for the accounts set aside for them is now up to twelve thousand pounds each."

"Why is there a disparity in the accounts, Papa?"

"Long ago, Jane, I began investing a certain amount for each child as it was born. Since you are the eldest yours has had more time to grow than theirs. By the time they are ready to marry, theirs will probably equal yours. Now Elizabeth has a little more in her account because she has invested money of her own from time to time. She has the funds I have invested plus another five thousand pounds that she invested. Since that had been added to what I invested she now has a total of twenty thousand pounds.

"What you girls have to decide is whether or not to count this money as your dowry or part of it only."

"I wish to count all of mine as my dowry, Papa. I think it will be for the best in our situation."

"Then it shall be as you say. Now Elizabeth, what say you."

"I will count five thousand pounds as my dowry and save the rest as it has been done in the past and receive it as you had originally planned."

"My Lizzy, you have chosen well. Gentlemen, add those amounts to the settlement papers."

Mr. Darcy looked proudly at his betrothed for making what he thought was a wise choice and the Colonel thought Jane had done the right thing for them, for the interest would come in handy when they married. He planned to sell out once he returned to London, and they had an estate to purchase. All in all everyone was quite satisfied.

To change the subject Jane said, "Papa, I think Mama has already been around the neighborhood with our news for Elizabeth and I have already received letters from congratulation from Meryton. I am upset that she let out the news before you had given your permission."

"I might have guessed she could not keep quiet, so we now have to make the best of it. Have you made any plans at all?"

"We have been talking among ourselves while you men were busy and we have made some decisions. One is that we wish to be married in London and we wish to plan our own weddings with no interference from mother. Elizabeth wants to have Georgiana stand up with her and I want Mary. We do not want mother trying to impose her will on our plans, so we ask you what we can do to forestall that?"

"My advice is to wait to tell her the date of the wedding until three days before you have planned for it. In that way she will not be thinking of what to do. Send a message to me and I will bring the others here for the weddings on the next day."

"Since Mary will stand up with me could you send her a little earlier so we can see to ordering her a gown?"

"I will send her ahead of the others. That should give you time to do what you must for her. Will you write her a note for me to take home with me?"

"Yes, I will write the note when you are ready to go home."

"May I suggest we choose a date now so we have something to work toward," suggested Mr. Darcy. "Miss Bennet and Elizabeth were scheduled to stay with Georgiana for two months and they have at least five more weeks ahead of them. I suggest a day in late October."

"How about the October 25, William?" suggested Elizabeth.

"Does that suit you two, Richard?"

"It suits me fine and by the looks from Jane, I think it suits her as well."

Now that they had a date they could plan other aspects of the wedding and Mr. Darcy offered to have the wedding breakfast at Darcy House in London. Then they made a list of those to invite to the wedding.

"Mr. Bennet, where do you plan to stay when you bring the rest of your family?"

"I believe it would be best to take them to a hotel. Otherwise my wife would be sticking her nose in everyone's business and I would not like to see her upset the brides."

"Since you think that would be best, I will not argue otherwise. I could, however, make arrangements for you at the Pulteny Hotel, which should make your wife more amendable. Georgie, I believe we ought to move the picnic to the nineteenth in order to facilitate our removal to London. Shall I send a note with a change on the invitation to that effect?"

"Yes, brother, that will be fine. It gives me time to plan and the Bennets can help with that.

Mr. Bennet, will you be able to stay with us until then?"

"I do not see why I could not. I will write to my wife and let her know of my plans."

CHAPTER FIVE

On the nineteenth the picnic for the Turners was held as planned. Mr. Turner was pleased to hear that his niece would soon be mistress of Pemberly and he knew that meant he would see more of his sister.

Everyone had a wonderful time playing games planned by Georgiana and partaking of the delectable food she had ordered. To top off the meal, Mr. Turner had brought some sweets from his shop to share with everyone. The Turner family went home with plenty of stories of the wonderful time they had to tell their neighbors.

On the twenty-first they all began their journey to London, filling two carriages and one coach with the luggage, passengers and servants going there. There were six passengers in the coach and the servants used Mr. Bennet's carriage. The first day was a lovely day for traveling for they would enjoy the changing color of the leaves as they bowled down the highways. A drizzling rain accompanied them the second day and it did not stop until they stopped for the night. They did not have so far to go on the third day so they arrived in London just after the noon hour.

Mr. Darcy insisted they all stay at Darcy House until the weddings, and despite Mr. Bennet's protest that is what they would do. So they arrived where servants came out in waves to gather the luggage and take it to the assigned rooms. The butler, Mr. Clark, and the housekeeper, Mrs. Mercer, met them at the door and the housekeeper showed the ladies to their rooms. Jane and Elizabeth had been assigned a suite of rooms near Georgiana's room and Mr. Bennet was assigned one across the hall from the ladies. The Colonel stayed in his usual room.

In his room, Mr. Bennet sat down and wrote a letter to Mr. Gardiner, telling him they had arrived in town. He then refreshed himself and went on back down the stairs to the drawing room to wait for his daughters. He planned to stay but a few more days before going back home, but he wanted to see his girls well settled first. At home he knew he would have a difficult time placating his wife, but it had to be done to keep his two favorite daughters happy.

At four that afternoon tea was served in the drawing room. They had been happily sipping their tea and exclaiming over their accommodations when some visitors were announced to Mr. Darcy. He was of a mind to refuse them, but they had already followed the butler into the room.

"Charles, I was not expecting you today, was I?"

"No, not at all, Darcy. Caroline noticed the empty carriages being taken to the mews and thought we should welcome you back to London. As you know, I could not stop her."

"I see you have the Bennets here. That is a surprise, I am sure," said Miss Bingley. "What brings them to Darcy House?"

"Allow me to introduce you to my betrothed, Miss Elizabeth Bennet and her sister, my cousin's betrothed, Miss Jane Bennet. And I believe you may already know Mr. Bennet."

Miss Caroline Bingley was struck by the announcement. For years she wished she had been in the position to be introduced as Mr. Darcy's betrothed. What in the world did he see in the daughter of a country gentleman of no account in the world?

Mr. Bennet could not help himself, but asked, "Mr. Bingley, you seemed to have moved out of Netherfield in quite a hurry, did you not?"

Mr. Bingley blushed, "I had some important business to conduct and have not had the opportunity to return to Hertfordshire. I dare say estate management is not my forte. I believe my sister and I must be going now."

They left as Mr. Darcy followed them out. Bingley, I am sure you know that I am not accustomed to receiving guests without further notice. I hope you will remember that in the future."

"Of course, I shall remember it well enough. I am sure Caroline will no longer wish to bother you, will you Caroline?"

"I am happy to hear that. And from this day forward you may not presume to go to an event by giving my name as a recommendation. I shall spread the word of my engagement as soon as may be and it would not look right for you to behave in such a manner, would it?

"And another thing, if I hear you have said one disparaging thing about my wife or her family, I will find it in me to cut you from my acquaintance completely."

In the Bingley coach, Mr. Bingley took a deep breath. "That was a surprise. I had no idea Darcy knew the Bennets, but they seemed to be as thick as thieves tonight."

"Nor did I, Charles. I am utterly astonished."

"Be sure you mind your tongue in future. I do not care to lose Darcy's friendship over this."

In the drawing room no one said a word about the intruders, but they continued to discuss what would need to be done in the next few weeks. The men's marching orders were to discuss financial matters with their solicitors, go to the church to secure it for the twenty-fifth of October, and to order that the banns be read beginning the first Sunday in October.

The women would arrange the shopping trips with Mrs. Gardiner and Lady Matlock and Georgiana would speak to Mrs. Mercer about the wedding breakfast. Richard took the time to write to his parents to let them know they were in town now and would welcome an audience with them. He sent the message by way of one of the Darcy servants and he brought back a reply in the affirmative, saying they would meet with Richard and the others after dinner.

Elizabeth sent a message to Mr. and Mrs. Gardiner and explained what their plans were for the next few days. She also invited them to come for after dinner teatime that evening.

In the meantime everyone was given a tour of the house from basement to attic. Not everyone wanted to see the attics, but Mr. Darcy wanted to show Elizabeth something that had been stored there since his mother died. He had brought a couple of lanterns with him so they could see better and he set them down near an old trunk. He pulled out the trunk and opened it so show what was inside. Therein were a number of bolts of fabric in brocades, silks, muslins, cottons, and the sheerest of laces and netting.

"Why would all of this be left up here? It is exquisite."

"My mother purchased these before she died. She planned to make some new gowns after Georgiana was born. But it was not to be. Now I want you to have them to do with as you will."

"I can already think of what to do with the silks and netting, but I shall not tell you yet. The muslins and cottons will make up into some lovely day gowns and the brocade can be used to replace some worn chair covers. Thank you so much."

"I knew you would know what to do with it. Shall I have a footman bring it downstairs for you?"

"Yes, please do. I think my aunt would like to see these fabrics. She has such a good eye for them."

"I am looking forward to meeting your Aunt and Uncle for it was with them I often saw you when you were in town."

"I am sure they would be pleased to meet you as well."

"Come, let us go downstairs and join the others."

They went downstairs and Mr. Darcy gave the order for the trunk to be brought to Elizabeth's room. It was at that time that the bell was rung signaling is was time to get ready for dinner, which sent everyone scurrying to their rooms to freshen up. They met again in the drawing room some forty-five minutes later and waited there for the dinner to be announced. Apparently the butler arrived not a moment to soon, for the Colonel announced he was starving.

Fortunately, there was enough food on the table to satisfy the hungry soldier and everyone else as well. At the end of the meal they agreed by mutual assent to forego the division of the sexes so they all went to the drawing room to await the arrival of their relatives.

Mr. Bennet drifted off to the library and was not seen again until bedtime, at which time he carried to his room five volumes.

The guests arrived almost simultaneously, the one carriage preceding the other by a few minutes. When one was emptied of its passengers and pulled off the other pulled up and was emptied of its passengers. The Matlocks were the first to ring the doorbell and were let in when the Gardiners reached the front doorway. The butler let everyone in and maids took their coats and hats and the butler led them to the drawing room to announce them.

They were greeted warmly by their families and introduced to each other and were soon talking of the weddings among them. Mr. Gardiner looked at Elizabeth and asked, "Will someone tell us what happened at Pemberley? We seem to have gotten a very simple report of the incident."

Colonel Fitzwilliam told them the whole story and the resultant consequences were that Mr. Wickham had stood trial in Derby and was sentenced to life on the colony in India. "My cousin was not injured at all, but Elizabeth had a few bruises and some powder burns on her hand caused by the report from the gun."

"Had it not been for Elizabeth's quick wits and analytical skills things could have turned out much worse than they did. She figured out the possibilities and was prepared for anything to happen," added Mr. Darcy.

"Oh, yes, our niece does have a quick wit about her. She has proven it to us on many an occasion," offered Mr. Gardiner.

Mr. Bennet was summoned to meet the Matlocks and greet the Gardiners. He came directly and spoke to the men in one corner while the women gathered in another one. What the men discussed was anybody's guess but the women were discussing what was uppermost in heir minds, the plans for shopping trips for two trousseaux. Mr. Gardiner and Lady Matlock divided their responsibilities, Lady Matlock was to manage Jane's needs and Mrs. Gardiner to do the same for Elizabeth. They would clear the better part of a week for their expeditions. The women would no doubt be invited to any number of teas when the news reached the newspapers.

Lady Matlock suggested giving a ball for the day before the weddings; by then the brides to be were beginning to feel a little overwhelmed. Mrs. Gardiner eased their minds by saying that everything would turn out fine for they had time enough to get everything done.

Elizabeth invited all of the ladies to go to her room to examine what was in the trunk. They had a gay old time touching the fabrics and deciding what to do with each piece. Mrs. Gardiner held out one silk that she thought would look well on Elizabeth and she said it was the color she wanted for her wedding gown. They put that one aside to take to the dressmakers on their first outing. Another piece would do well for Georgiana's gown, and yet one more for Jane. Being so well ahead of the game eased everyone's mind. They also found a fabric that would do for Mary's gown, so Mr. Bennet would take that home with him and have the gown made in Meryton.

On the first day of shopping the modiste was quite satisfied with the fabrics brought to her. She found a piece of the sheer fabric Elizabeth wanted as an overskirt. She helped the girls chose fabric for a number of other gowns and they ordered what they wanted and went on to another shop to order undergarments and the like. The next items to order were the ball gowns for everyone, so Elizabeth chose another piece of fabric to send home with her father to make a ball gown for Mary.

Satisfied with their first day of shopping they went home to rest before they did another thing that day. The men came home a half an hour after the ladies, having completed all of their tasks. They were happy to hear the ladies had a good day and were pleased with their choices.

What gave Mr. Darcy the most joy was that Elizabeth would be wearing fabric chosen by his mother. He felt it afforded a connection to the family in some tangible way Elizabeth would not have otherwise had. He knew he was lucky to have finally found her and she had agreed to be his wife, for she was everything he had hoped she would be. He felt the next few weeks would not go fast enough to suit him, but he would be as patient as he could be for the duration of the wait.

For Elizabeth and Jane the time passed more quickly because of the incessant calls for them to go in for final fittings of some garments. This also included the number of teas held after the news spread through town. Lady Matlock chose which ones to attend and which ones to refuse.

Both girls would now be members of significant families and they would have to ready for anything that came before them. It would take longer for Jane to become acclimated to her new life, but Elizabeth was so outgoing she would fare better. She could hold her own in various conversations because of her educational background. Her opinions had merit and it did not take long for society to realize she could take all that was dished out to her with aplomb. Many respected her for this and for those who did not, but it mattered not to her for she was not a social climber.

Mr. Bingley steered clear of Jane whenever they attended the same events. It seems he was embarrassed about his actions the past year and in some way he regretted it. Jane was beautiful, sweet and poised, something his sister Caroline had not mastered for all her finishing school training and being out in society for so long. The Bennets paid no mind to the Bingleys but did speak on occasion to Mr. and Mrs. Hurst. In time they became better acquainted and would be accepted at Darcy House if not at Matlock House.

On a day before the weddings, Mrs. Hurst visited and brought Caroline with her. Elizabeth and Jane were wearing one of their new gowns that day and were all that was charming and gracious. They looked he part of the upper circle. They stood to greet the visitors and bade them to sit down. After going over the usual inanities, Caroline began to relate what she had come to say.

"Miss Bennet, Miss Elizabeth, I should like to apologize for my unkind words when we were all in Hertfordshire. I have come to realize it was wrong of me to say those untrue things about you both. Can you forgive me?"

"Miss Bingley, if you are truly repentant, I can forgive you," responded Jane in her usual gracious manner.

Elizabeth thought a moment to form the correct response. Since she had been the brunt of more of the criticism she had more to forgive. "Miss Bingley, I feel I can forgive you, but it will be long time before I can forget all that you had said and done. I think we should be civil to each other in public but at this time I will need continual proof of the sincerity of your apology. It is the best I can do at this time and at a later date we could readdress the issue. The rest is up to you to improve your manners toward those you believe to be beneath you."

"I quite understand all that you have said. I realize I overstepped by bounds and I know both of you are daughters of a gentleman and above me socially. I do not want there to enmity between our families in the future."

"Very well, we shall go on as we have described and who knows, we may become good friends by then. It was good of you to make the effort and I recognize it cannot have been easy. I could only wish now that your brother would apologize to Jane for his neglect when he left so suddenly, leaving her to face the derision of the neighborhood. Also I would not wish to interfere in the friendship between your brother and Mr. Darcy. I would not wish for them to be at odds. Of course, it is up to him to take the necessary steps to come to a reconciliation with my family."

"Perhaps we should have some tea now," suggested Jane.

"Thank you, we would love to have some tea," responded Mrs. Hurst.

Jane ordered the tea and before it came Mr. Darcy and Georgiana entered the drawing room, having finished their morning tasks. Mr. Darcy noted Caroline sitting there and was about to say something, but Elizabeth walked up to him and put her hand on his arm. "My dear, Miss Bingley has come to apologize to

Jane and me for some offenses enacted against us in Hertfordshire. We have forgiven her for those offenses and I hope you may do likewise."

"I shall give it some consideration, my love. Shall we be seated?"

They sat down and Caroline said, "Mr. Darcy, I have apologized to both Miss Bennet and Miss Elizabeth. Now I wish to make amends with you."

"If my dear lady has forgiven you, I can only support her wishes. However, you may be assured I will not tolerate any more of your behaviors, neither against them or any of their family."

"You have my word that I will not repeat such behaviors. I did not realize the connection to your family."

"Miss Bingley, whether or not the Bennets are connected to my family, it was wrong of you to judge them on first impressions. You must become more discerning," said Mr. Darcy.

The tea tray came in and Georgiana prepared the tea for everyone there. Mrs. Hurst asked Jane and Elizabeth when the wedding would be and they told her the date. Jane said, "We have finished our trousseau shopping and the plans are already done for us. Our father and mother and our other sisters will be here by Wednesday. They will have rooms in a hotel while they are in town. Mary will be here tomorrow for she will stand up with me and Georgiana will stand up for Elizabeth.

"The Matlock's younger son, Andrew, will stand up with the Colonel and my uncle will stand up with Mr. Darcy."

"Will Lady de Bourgh attend the wedding?"

"We are not certain because her daughter is ill and we have not heard if she has become well, Miss Bingley. I am sure Lady Catherine would not want to leave her daughter alone at home."

"Of course, I understand that. Louisa it is time for us to leave now. I am sure Miss Bennet and Miss Elizabeth have much to do this week."

The two ladies left and wondered whether they made any difference in the feelings of the others, which was still to be determined. Caroline would now do her best to make amends and urge her brother to apologize to Jane for abandoning her to the derision of the populace in Meryton. It would do her no good to be at odds with the Darcy family, and she knew she had to make good on her apology.

CHAPTER SIX

Mary arrived on time to join the afternoon tea. She was taken to her room to refresh herself and joined everyone for tea in the drawing room while the maid assigned to her emptied her trunk. She was introduced to Mr. Darcy, the now Mr. Fitzwilliam, and Miss Georgiana. They all tried to make Mary feel at home with them and she began to feel at ease there.

She went to her first event the next day at the Matlocks to have their afternoon tea. The whole family was there to meet Mary and one in particular sought her out and spoke to her exclusively.

For the days before the rest of the family arrived, Jane, Elizabeth, Georgiana and Mary spent most of their time together. Mary did not pick up Fordyce's Sermons even once during that time.

The day came for Mr. Bennet to come to town with his wife and other two daughters. Coming with them in another carriage were Mr. and Mrs. Philips. They stopped for a short while at Darcy House and Mrs. Bennet was speechless for a while. Mrs. Philips stored up all she saw as much as possible and it would not take long before all she saw would be spread around in Meryton.

Kitty was as stunned as her mother, and Lydia had to touch everything she laid her eyes on. She asked to borrow Elizabeth's ball gown when she saw it, and Elizabeth said it would not fit her. She and Kitty could not go to the ball anyway. Mary was the only one invited to the ball, because she was in the wedding party. Lydia mourned that it was not fair that they were to be left out. Her father told her she was not fit to be seen in high society. Kitty seemed to understand the restrictions placed on the younger set.

To make them feel a little better, Mr. Darcy had arranged to take them to Vauxhall Gardens on the next evening. On that day the party consisted of Mr. and Mrs. Bennet, Mr. Darcy and Elizabeth, Mr. Fitzwilliam and Jane, Mary and Anthony, the youngest Fitzwilliam Pauline, Georgina, Kitty and Lydia. The four youngest stayed together and everyone was satisfied with their placements. Georgiana and Pauline were perfectly capable of keeping Lydia in line the whole time. They were good examples of deportment for the twins.

Georgiana kept Kitty entertained with her explanation of all the treats that were in store for the party. They would see a play and a musical and at the end a fireworks display. The evening would be topped off with a supper prepared for them in a private box.

Mrs. Bennet was her usual self that night and Elizabeth felt the embarrassment on more than one occasion. The older woman had formed the intention of creating a relationship between Lydia and Anthony. That would certainly make an ill-suited couple if she succeeded. What the woman did not know was that Anthony had already chosen another for himself and there was nothing Mrs. Bennet could say about Lydia that would sway him.

Mr. Darcy noticed Elizabeth's unease about her mother and said, "My dearest Elizabeth, you need not be concerned about your mother's behavior. We all have family members who embarrass us from time to time. When compared to my Aunt Catherine your mother is harmless and means no one any ill will. Anthony knows his own mind and if he wishes to choose one of your sisters, nothing will move him from his decision, and I think he has already made up his mind."

"I shall try not to be bothered so much by my mother's pronouncements. I know how she can be and I know she speaks without thinking. It is unfortunate that my father has not seen fit to correct her behaviors in all these years and I suppose he never will. He is the same in regards to supervising Kitty and Lydia. I only wish that I shall do better when I have children."

"I have no doubt that you will be an excellent mother."

"I think you will be an exemplary father."

Mr. Darcy chuckled and took her hand and kissed it.

It was the day after the trip to Vauxhall that the ball was held. That day the ladies spent a good part of it preparing themselves for the evening. They washed their hair, had it dried and styled and ate a light meal brought to them on trays to suffice them until the supper hour at the dance. They donned their gowns one hour before they were to leave. Jane and Elizabeth wore stylish gowns in silk and Mary wore one in fine muslin, for she was still too young to wear the silk that Jane and Elizabeth could wear. Their slippers matched their gowns and each of them wore elbow length gloves to cover the exposed skin on their arms.

Elizabeth wore a string of pearls entwined in her hair and Jane wore rosebuds in her hair. Mary had her hair styled without adornment, but she wore Elizabeth's garnet necklace. She looked very pretty beside her sisters in her new hairstyle and gown.

When it was time to go to the ball, Georgiana looked them over critically and could find nothing out of order. She told them they would be the most beautiful of all the ladies in attendance.

Georgiana was allowed to go because she was a member of the Fitzwilliam family, but she would not be able to dance, and would have to go to her room after the supper. She would be staying at the Matlock's home that night and while the bridal couples were away on their wedding trips.

During the ball, the brides and Mary met many new people, some who were good friends of the Fitzwilliams and Mr. Darcy. The Hursts and Bingleys were not there because they were not friends of the hosts and no one seemed to miss them. Mr. and Mrs. Bennet were there, but Mr. and Mrs. Philips stayed with the girls at the hotel.

Mrs. Bennet was awed by all of the splendor in the ballroom. Chandeliers sparkled like diamonds and bouquets of flowers were stationed on tables between the windows along one wall, with candles on either side of the vases. Her husband stayed by her to forestall any lapses in deportment. Even though, he had to problem speaking to those he met.

Elizabeth got on well with those she met, charming them with her wit and superior knowledge. Jane did well as long as her betrothed stayed with her. She was much shyer than her sister. Both of them had full dance cards, and at the end of the evening they found that Mary had a full dance card as well.

At the supper hour, Mr. Bennet, Lord Matlock, Andrew Fitzwilliam and Mr. Darcy's good friend the Duke of Monmouth offered toasts for the bridal couples. The Duke was at the ball with his young wife, Anna, who found

Elizabeth to be a wonderful conversationalist and invited her to call on her when she was back from her wedding trip. In time she was sure Elizabeth and she would become very good friends.

The second half of the ball saw some of the guests leave early to rest before the wedding the next day, but the bridal party had to stay until the very end of the festivities. Mr. Darcy and his party slipped out just after the last set of dances in order to get home in good time. The weddings were scheduled for ten in the morning and that meant everyone had to be ready in a timely manner.

In truth it was an exhausted party that climbed into bed that night. Not a peep was heard from them until the maids and valets came to wake them with aromatic cups of tea, coffee, and chocolate. Elizabeth and Jane had two maids tending to them, seeing that they were bathed and refreshed for the day. After donning shifts, stays and petticoats, the maids worked on the brides' hair. By nine they had to step into their gowns and have them fastened.

Downstairs Mr. Bennet awaited his daughters' presence. Mary came down first and a maid helped her into her cape. Now it was time for the brides to descend the stairs, and Mr. Bennet was so proud of his daughters. Both of them were beautiful in their bridal array and a tear came to his eye. He brushed it away and when they approached him, he kissed them on the cheek. He helped them into the carriage and climbed in himself, and in twenty more minutes they were pulling up in front of the church. A servant came out to assist them from the carriage and lead them into the foyer of the building. Inside Georgiana was waiting for them. The capes were handed to the servant and he put them in an anteroom. Mary and Georgiana shook out the skirts for the brides, and then shook their own skirts. Mary placed the veil over Elizabeth's head and arranged it charmingly.

Now they were ready for the sound of the march music. Mary and Georgiana were to precede the brides, and then Mr. Bennet would escort the brides down the aisle, Jane on his left and Elizabeth on his right. The music began and the attendants began their walk down the aisle. When they reached the altar and took their places, Mr. Bennet and the brides began their walk. All eyes were on them, the most important ones looking at them with love and devotion.

While the ceremony was underway, the activity at the Darcy House kitchen was intensive and had been since the day before. Servants scurried here and there seeing to all the arrangements and checking for the fourth time that everything was in place. At the designated time, platters of delectable foods were brought out to be staged so the servants could dish the food out onto plates to be delivered to the diners.

Crystal wine glasses twinkled and snowy white tablecloths covered tables. The whole ballroom was filled with these tables, allowing eight to ten to fit at each one. Name cards were at each setting and the chairs were positioned exactly the same at each table. Numerous footmen in dress livery gathered in the servants' hall, at the ready to perform their duties. Maids were dressed in the very best uniforms as well.

Back at the church the vows had been spoken, the mothers cried, and if anyone cared to look, so did the fathers. Georgiana and Mary also shed a few tears as they returned down the aisle to the front of the church where the registry book was placed. The bridal couples followed them along with the parents of one groom and the parents of the brides. They signed all the register and called for the outerwear, while the rest of the attendees rushed for the carriages to go to the wedding breakfast. A veritable caravan of carriages followed the road into Berkeley Square to Mr. Darcy's home.

The bridal party took a short cut to the house and was able to go to the mews and walk to the house and enter the back way and into the ballroom. By doing so they were there to meet the guests as the arrived to find their tables and be seated. The bridal couples were seated at their own table with the attendants. The families were at tables nearby. When all were seated the signal was given for the servants to start bringing out the filled plates.

Toasts were given liberally throughout the ballroom and everyone had a lively time due to the contingent of military gentlemen who were invited. The whole meal lasted for two hours and the brides and grooms were eager to be away to start their new lives. Jane and the Colonel were the first to leave, but Mr. Darcy and Elizabeth were obliged to stay until every last guest had gone home.

When they finally were alone, except for the servants, they were able to go to their rooms and change into their traveling clothes. Before they left their rooms, Mr. Darcy took the opportunity to kiss his wife thoroughly, something he had wanted to do since he had proposed. They then left for a trip to lakes, a place Elizabeth had been longing to see for quite some time, where they had the time to learn more about each other. In the long run they were a very compatible couple.

EPILOG

They did not return to Pemberly for six weeks. By then Georgiana had arrived and met them as they entered the house. She was happy to see them and they were glad to be home.

They spent the winter in Derbyshire and did not go to London until March to spend the last of the season there and to catch up on the activities of friends and family. By that time Jane was increasing and so was Elizabeth so they had much to discuss about the growth of their families.

Andrew Fitzwilliam had continued to be interested in Mary and asked his brother if he could invite her to come to London for a time so that he could court her properly. Richard did so and it was not long before Mary came and not much longer before she was engaged. They married two months later at Lord Matlock's estate. The couple resided in London where Andrew had work at the Bank of London.

Other Books by this Author

60608159R00086

Made in the USA
Middletown, DE
02 January 2018